"How dare you," Evonne panted

Her desperate struggle to free herself was useless. "How dare you climb into my room!"

"I didn't do it from choice, believe me," Rick said ironically. "It was the only way to get to you—to break into your ivory tower."

When he released her abruptly, she sat down awkwardly on the bed. She glared at him resentfully, full of so many conflicting emotions she couldn't speak.

"What happened back there?" He gestured toward the main complex.

"Nothing."

"Don't lie, Evonne," he said curtly. "One moment you were having the time of your life, the next you were running for cover. Did you suddenly realize how much you've broken your vows lately, that you were living and laughing—and loving it?"

LINDSAY ARMSTRONG married an accountant from New Zealand and settled down—if you can call it that—in Australia. A coast-to-coast camping trip later, they moved to a six-hundred-acre mixed-grain property, which they eventually abandoned to the mice and leeches and black flies. Then, after a winning career at the track with an untried trotter, purchased "mainly because he had blue eyes," they opted for a more conventional family life with their five children in Brisbane, where Lindsay now writes.

Books by Lindsay Armstrong

HARLEQUIN PRESENTS
559—MELT A FROZEN HEART
607—ENTER MY JUNGLE
806—SAVED FROM SIN
871—FINDING OUT
887—LOVE ME NOT
927—AN ELUSIVE MISTRESS
951—SURRENDER MY HEART
983—STANDING ON THE OUTSIDE
1039—THE SHADOW OF MOONLIGHT
1071—RELUCTANT WIFE
1095—WHEN YOU LEAVE ME
1183—HEAT OF THE MOMENT

HARLEQUIN ROMANCE
2443—SPITFIRE
2497—MY DEAR INNOCENT
2582—PERHAPS LOVE
2653—DON'T CALL IT LOVE
2785—SOME SAY LOVE
2876—THE HEART OF THE MATTER
2893—WHEN THE NIGHT GROWS COLD
3013—THE MARRYING GAME

Don't miss any of our special offers. Write to us at the following address for information on our newest releases.

Harlequin Reader Service
901 Fuhrmann Blvd., P.O. Box 1397, Buffalo, NY 14240
Canadian address: P.O. Box 603,
Fort Erie, Ont. L2A 5X3

LINDSAY ARMSTRONG

one more night

Harlequin Books

TORONTO • NEW YORK • LONDON
AMSTERDAM • PARIS • SYDNEY • HAMBURG
STOCKHOLM • ATHENS • TOKYO • MILAN

Harlequin Presents first edition September 1990
ISBN 0-373-11295-5

Original hardcover edition published in 1989
by Mills & Boon Limited

CHAPTER ONE

Amos Doubleday leant back in his chair with his hands forming a steeple on his rather rotund stomach and contemplated the ceiling.

Evonne Patterson, who was sitting opposite him across the wide polished expanse of his beautiful teak desk, waited patiently. In the two years that she had worked for Amos as his personal assistant and advertising liaison officer she had come to respect his contemplative silences. Not only that, she found herself musing as she waited. His extremely shrewd brain and marketing instinct, which had helped him to form a chain of exclusive department stores down the eastern seaboard of Australia, had inspired her admiration, and to have helped achieve another of his pet dreams gave her cause for great satisfaction. For Amos had not been content to let matters rest with his successful chain of stores. He had had a dream—or perhaps a mania— about catalogues. 'Not just any catalogue,' he'd said vehemently to Evonne when he'd interviewed her. 'Not just a piece of junk mail people throw away without looking at and get mad at because they clutter up their mail boxes. I want ours to be *the* state of the art catalogue, a quarterly catalogue so beautifully presented, so exquisitely contrived, so full of marvellous merchandise that people drool over it, treasure it even...can you visualise what I have in mind?'

Evonne had blinked, then said slowly that she thought she could. Whereupon Amos had subjected her person, her long dark hair, her dark eyes and pale skin, her figure beneath the camellia-pink linen suit she wore, her glossy lips and nails that matched exactly, her pale patterned stockings and beautiful calf shoes, to an unblinking stare for a full minute, then he had said thoughtfully that he thought she might just be the epitome of the kind of taste he had in mind—and had offered her the job.

Over the succeeding two years, they had not only realised his dream but formed a rapport. 'We're a lot alike, you know, Evonne,' Amos was fond of saying frequently, and occasionally adding with a wink, 'I just wish I were twenty-five years younger!' He was in fact happily married to an equally rotund, homely little lady whose great cross in life was that she had been unable to bear Amos any children. Evonne knew this, and she accepted these occasional remarks as a tribute from an older and basically kindly man. She also had to agree with him when he said, having gleaned some knowledge of her background, 'We're tough and we're bright and tenacious, you and I. We've made it from almost nothing—look at you! Barely twenty-eight and a highly successful business executive.'

Yes, Evonne thought, on a cold, grey Melbourne summer morning when the sun should have been shining but, in true fickle Melbourne manner, was not, and Amos was composing his thoughts, I've come a long way from the back streets of Woolloomooloo, a Sydney slum then. Such a long way... I just wish I felt more of a sense of achievement.

'Yes,' said Amos, sitting up and lowering his gaze from the ceiling, 'I've thought it through and I've come to the conclusion that you're the only person I can entrust this mission with.' He stared at Evonne earnestly.

'Mission?' She raised an eyebrow.

Amos coughed delicately. 'You know Hattie and I have never had any kids—which we accept as the will of God, but,' he shrugged, 'well, my sister was more blessed. She had a boy—she married a galloping Pommie and they had this boy.' He paused.

Evonne waited, speculating idly on what a galloping Pommie could possibly be but knowing that in his own time Amos would enlighten her.

'That's one of the things I've always liked about you, Evonne,' her boss continued. 'You can be a very quiet, still, restful woman. You don't immediately bombard me with questions, you wait and you think. His father was a diplomat and they've lived all over the world, which is not necessarily a good way to bring up children.'

'I see,' Evonne murmured.

'Yes, because the boy now has a restless soul, I'm afraid, and can't settle to anything. He's spent the last year living in Papua New Guinea, studying the natives—I'm not sure if he sees himself as a budding anthropologist or archaeologist or what, but that's what he's been doing, and, heaven forbid, he's written this book.'

Evonne's lips quirked. 'Heaven forbid?'

'Well,' said Amos with a large gesture, 'I personally am not all that interested in head-hunters and the strange rituals of primitive persons, nor, I suspect,' his brown eyes gleamed shrewdly, 'am I the only one.'

'So you don't see it being a best-seller, exactly?'

'It has to be a limited market even if it's a good book, don't you agree?'

Evonne considered and answered obliquely, 'We seem to have been inundated with that kind of thing lately, not only in the form of books but television . . .'

'Exactly!' Amos broke in triumphantly.

'All the same, it's quite an achievement for a boy . . .'

'Not precisely a boy, he's a young man now, I suppose you would say,' Amos interrupted again, a little hastily, and added worriedly, 'and of course, you know what young men are like— hot-headed, idealistic, *rash* . . .'

'Amos,' said Evonne with a faint grin, 'I'm sorry to have to desert my quiet, restful image, but I'm about to ask a question. Are you leading up to . . .'

'Wait just a minute!' he commanded. 'Let me explain fully. *Because* Hattie and I have no children—we have no one to leave all this to!' he finished like a conjuror pulling a rabbit out of a hat.

'I . . . think I begin to see,' Evonne said slowly.

'I knew you would. When I say no one . . .'

'You do have your...er...sister's boy.'

'Exactly, *but* if he has no interest, no training, no background, I might as well not waste my time.'

'Amos, from what you've told me about him, if you're thinking of trying to mould him into taking all this over you could be wasting your time anyway.'

'He's *young*,' he said intensely. 'How often do we know what we want when we're young? I myself had some curious ambitions when I was young, although to be honest, enquiring into the sexual practices of the Kukukukus was not one of them, but to each his own... At least I can try, though. Hattie is with me on this,' he added steadfastly.

'Well,' Evonne smiled at him affectionately, 'why not, then? But when are you going to tell me where I fit in? I must warn you, nothing would induce me to go among the Kukukukus, and I really don't see...'

'Brampton Island,' Amos said succinctly.

She frowned.

'You know the Whitsundays? Sea, sand, coral...'

'I know where Brampton Island is,' Evonne said coolly.

'*He's* there, my sister's boy—recuperating. He broke his ankle a few weeks back.'

'Amos...'

'Evonne, it would be like a holiday for you. All I'm asking is that you help him get his notes——'

'I thought it was a full-blown book.'

'It *will* be—with your help. It's all there, he tells me, just in a bit of...disarray,' Amos said smoothly. 'You know how good you are at organising things—why, it's that talent, and of course your marvellous taste, that makes you invaluable to me!'

'Amos, I'm allergic to blackmail, and this is not what you employed me for—a good secretary could do it.'

'A good secretary couldn't do what I have in mind,' countered Amos. 'Getting his book into shape is not my aim, my *main* aim. Let me explain. Here we have a young man who's flouted convention to an extent; he's roamed far, done something rather different, come close to quite an achievement—I don't want to take that away from him! But if there's the possibility that he's not *set* in *that* mould, and I do honestly see it more as a sowing of his wild oats, then he could now be ripe for something different—and if he's inherited a tenth of his mother's genes, which were very similar to mine, this,' he dabbed a forefinger at the desk quite forcefully, 'is his milieu. As it is yours,' he added sternly. 'So who better than you to woo him into seeing it this way?'

Exasperation and amusement warred for expression in Evonne. 'You make me sound like some sort of seductress!' she protested.

'You are. You are,' Amos said vigorously. 'Just to look at you is to be seduced—not that I expect you for one minute to *actually* seduce him, I doubt if he's your type at all, besides the generation gap, but the magic of this business flows in you like a quiet river, raises it from mere commerce to an art! Just to know you, to hear you talk about your work, can't *fail* to make an impression on him.'

'Amos...'

'And you know what young people are like,' Amos continued indulgently. 'They'd far rather believe a perfect stranger than their own flesh and blood.'

'Yes, well,' said Evonne, 'I have to confess that when you flatter me as you just have, I tend to get suspicious.'

'Suspicious? I'm deeply hurt,' Amos replied, but his brown eyes twinkled all the same. Then he sighed and sobered. 'Hattie has rather set her heart on this. You know how I can never deny her anything, even though I told her it might not work out. Would...say some weeks of your time, on full pay, naturally, be such an imposition, my friend?' He stared at her steadily.

She hesitated.

'We're in for a rotten summer, so they tell us, and it would be warm up there. Look,' he gestured to the window upon which spears of rain were now falling. 'Also, we've finalised the next catalogue and in my opinion it's a masterpiece, but you're looking a bit tired, if I may say so. And there's nothing else of importance coming up—apart from the Anniversary Dinner, but you've been to a couple of those. Incidentally, I've also finalised the guest list. Care to comment?' He slid a piece of paper across the desk to her.

Evonne picked it up and glanced through it desultorily, her mind still occupied with Amos's fantastic proposition. Then she stiffened barely perceptibly and raised her eyes to his.

'You're inviting the Randalls?'

'Should I not?' He spread his hands. 'I knew Robert Randall's grandfather quite well, and Narelle Kingston, his mother-in-law—well, she's remarried now but she's been a valued client for a long time. Didn't you like him? I must say he gave you an excellent reference when you left him.'

'I...it's not...no, I didn't dislike him,' Evonne said, unusually disjointedly, and winced inwardly. 'I . . .'

'Did you ever meet his wife? They say she's charming.'

'She is. She . . . is.'

'Well then?' Amos looked perplexed.

'Nothing,' Evonne said hurriedly. 'How long did you have in mind my babysitting your sister's boy for?'

He sat back. 'I wouldn't quite call it babysitting—as long as it takes to get his notes into reasonable manuscript form. Naturally I'd also pay all your expenses.'

'Will we be on Brampton all the time?'

He lifted his shoulders carelessly. 'Wherever the whim takes you—I give you *carte blanche*. I believe he has some sort of an arrangement to meet an editor of some sort in Sydney in the near future.'

Evonne studied her boss thoughtfully, even though she knew she *would* take on this impossible-sounding assignment. She said, 'I'll give it three weeks.' That would take her safely past the Anniversary Dinner.

'Evonne...'

'Three weeks, Amos. You'll have to trust me to know whether it's a lost cause in that time. And that's my last offer,' she added with a wry smile.

'Done!' he said immediately, and opened a drawer from which he extracted an airline ticket folder that he pushed across the desk to her. 'Now don't be annoyed with me,' he said as her smile faded. 'It's just that I knew I could count on you to help me out in something that means so much to me and Hattie.'

Evonne opened her mouth, but closed it as she thought that without Amos Doubleday and his passion for a perfect catalogue the past two years would have been sheer, unadulterated hell.

They eyed each other in silence until she said huskily, 'What's his name? You haven't told me that.'

Amos smiled radiantly at her. 'Emerson. Richard Carlisle Emerson—but we call him Ricky. Now why don't you take the afternoon off, pop downstairs to the Gone Troppo boutique and kit yourself out for the Whitsundays? Then you could leave tomorrow morning! I'll wire Ricky that you're coming.'

'I must be mad,' Evonne murmured to herself late that night as she sat at her elegant dining-room table in her elegant flat, composing a note for her cleaning lady to explain her forthcoming absence. This was not an unusual practice—she frequently made business trips at short notice and her gem of a cleaning lady could be relied upon to take care of such things as getting her paper and milk delivery stopped, her clothes to the dry-cleaners, her fridge relieved of anything likely to go off, etc.

Her bags were packed and waiting in the hall for an early getaway, her portable typewriter was there too... and all that remains, she reflected as she got up to stick the note on the fridge door with a magnet, is to formulate some sort of plan of action for coping with a budding David Attenborough whose very last intention probably is of following in his uncle's footsteps. I wonder how old he *is*? I haven't had anything to do with very young men for ages except my brother Sam, and he's nearly twenty-one now, and car- and girl-mad in that order. But Richard Carlisle Emerson doesn't sound quite like the run-of-the-mill young man, and he must be bright if he's written this book at such a tender age. He's probably earnest and eager—I wouldn't be at all surprised if he wears glasses and has damp palms and definite opinions...

She broke off her reflections to smile ruefully and decide that, for some strange reason, she already felt rather protective of young Ricky Emerson.

'Must be my maternal instincts coming to the fore,' she mused, and wandered into her bedroom and across to the window.

The skies had cleared and it was a starry night she looked out upon. And then, like a dam breaking, she found she could no longer hold back her thoughts and memories of Robert Randall, and she stood silent and shaking and foolishly clutching the curtain for support.

The next morning there were dark smudges beneath her eyes, testimony to a sleepless night, as she flew from Melbourne to Brisbane and on to Mackay in North Queensland. By the time she discovered she had only been put on the waiting list for the ten-minute Twin Otter flight to Brampton Island, that no cancellation had come up and she had over an hour to wait for the next flight, she had a headache to accompany her tiredness.

It was also hot, extremely hot, and the small terminal emptied of people almost magically, to slumber in the sunshine and humidity until the next crop of arrivals and departures. For a time Evonne wandered about inspecting the posters and pamphlets which almost all proclaimed Mackay as the gateway to the wonderland of the Great Barrier Reef and the Whitsunday Islands; and from force of long habit she gathered a few to familiarise herself with this world of resort islands, this playground of coral reefs, aquamarine waters, palm-fringed beaches—only to discover herself in the grip of a spiritual torpor that caused her to be wholly uninterested.

So she bought herself an orange juice, sat herself down to wait, and took herself severely to task. Think of young Ricky Emerson, she commanded herself, think of Amos and dear, sweet Hattie who's obviously pining to get her hands on *someone* she can mother, think of all your successes, the job offers, the enticements other firms offer you to lure you away from Amos, the career you've carved out so that you'll be fulfilled and active and sought after for a good long time...

Don't, whatever you do, look backwards, because you *have* survived when you thought you mightn't; you *can* cope, it's only when something actually reminds you nowadays...

Think of all you've been able to do for Mum and the others, think of your lovely flat, your car, your clothes...

A smile twisted her lips at last and she wondered if she wasn't really incurably shallow-minded, because where others might find solace in religion or music or art or whatever, clothes riveted her and always had. Also the kind of marvellous merchandise Amos filled his catalogues with—silverware and turquoise, china and porcelain, miniatures, leather especially embossed and tooled, crystal, pearls, lace, imported tartans, Oriental carpets so fine and silky you couldn't bear to walk on them, but clothes still came first—and now, thanks to Amos considering her a walking advertisement for his clothing departments, she didn't even have to buy them. And she remembered, with another slight smile, her first couturier suit and how she had scrimped and saved to buy it and then had to put it away for a few months until she could afford the shoes to do it justice—and lost weight in the process so that it had no longer been a perfect fit. She remembered how she had gradually built up a

wardrobe of good clothes, not extensive but skil-
fully integrated not only for financial reasons but
also because while one part of her soul was seduced by pure wool, linen, silk, crisp cotton, cuts,
styles, lines and subtle colours, another part of
her soul was frugal and cautious, and strangely,
those two elements rarely warred. Even today,
when she had a world of fashion at her fingertips, her wardrobe was still not large, but it suited
every occasion.

'Well, nearly,' she amended to herself, looking
down at her khaki linen pants and sage-green
blouse and fingering the wide tan leather belt
around her waist, all of which was clinging to her
damply or, in the case of the belt, grippingly. 'But
I suspect, in this climate, the less you wear the
better. It's just as well I visited the Gone Troppo
boutique and got myself a few really flimsy
pieces.' Then she jumped as someone touched her
on the shoulder and she looked up to see an
airline representative standing before her.

'Oh, I'm sorry, I was daydreaming!'

'So I gathered,' the man said with a grin. 'It's
Miss Patterson, isn't it? Your flight to Brampton
has landed and they'll be off again as soon as
you're aboard.'

'Am I the only passenger?' asked Evonne,
looking around.

'Today you are, but there's also some extra
baggage to go across. You'll still be there in time
for lunch, by the way.'

'Great! I'm...I'm hungry,' she said with some
surprise as she stood up and went with him
towards the tarmac, and he smiled at her again

as he took in her figure, the way she walked with a model's ease and grace, her glossy dark hair and beautiful skin, with the kind of admiration she was very used to seeing in men's eyes but had closed her heart to completely.

She discovered on the short flight across the water to the island that Brampton had in fact escaped Captain Cook's notice on his voyage of discovery up the east coast of Australia in the late seventeen-hundreds.

'Didn't miss much, the old boy,' the genial pilot said into the PA, 'but see this bigger island to the right of Brampton—we're actually passing between them now for our final descent—it hid Brampton from view.'

She also learned that Brampton was part of the Cumberland group of islands, that the resort had recently been rebuilt, a process that had not quite been completed, but most of the facilities were now very modern yet designed to blend with the landscape—and that she had a namesake on the island. A tame, very curious emu called Evonne, although it was possibly spelt with a Y.

For some reason or other, hearing this completed Evonne's (i.e. Patterson) as she thought of it in brackets, restoration. Her headache had gone, she discovered, she was still tired, but pleasantly so now, and filled with a mild sort of anticipation. Really, she thought, as they floated down to land and she looked down on to a vista of curved beach, sparkling sea, green, wooded hills, flowering trees and creepers, I might just enjoy this project after all.

*   *   *

'Yes, Mr . . . er . . . Mr Emerson did get a message that you were arriving, Miss . . . Miss Patterson,' the receptionist said to Evonne with a trace of confusion. 'He got a telegram from Melbourne, in fact, but . . . well, look, as soon as I can lay my hands on him, I'll let him know you're here. He's probably on the beach or gone in to lunch, but in the meantime, we've allocated you a room next door to his, and it's in a lovely spot, right on the beach. I'm sure you'll like it—also the opportunity to freshen up for lunch. Susan here, from Guest Liaison, will be your guide and show you the way. Your luggage should already be there now.'

'Thank you,' smiled Evonne, and started to turn away, then she turned back, 'Look, don't worry about tracking Mr Emerson down. If we're in next-door rooms, I'll catch up with him sooner or later. There's no urgency.'

'If you're sure?'

'Quite sure,' Evonne said definitely, thinking that she would allow young Ricky Emerson a further few hours of freedom and provide herself with the opportunity to further unwind at the same time.

Susan, whose job it was to help organise entertainment for guests, chatted charmingly as she led Evonne through the resort, pointing out places of interest at the same time. 'That's where they feed the rainbow lorikeets and demonstrate how to open coconuts. Those are the old Carlisle units which are due to be demolished very soon— you're in the new Blue Lagoon ones.'

'Carlisle?' queried Evonne with a lift of an eyebrow.

'It's the name of our twin island just across the channel, the one that hid Brampton from Captain Cook and Matthew Flinders—and this railway line we're crossing goes over to the Deepwater Jetty; it's a miniature train really and the only form of transport there, but it's fun. It meets all the boats that come in. Now these are the new Blue Lagoon units. They're different, aren't they?'

Evonne nodded in agreement as they wended their way along a flagged path between biscuit-coloured, steep-roofed, two-storeyed buildings, each containing eight rooms and surrounded by trees, shrubs and with exotic creepers trained up their walls. Different but rather nice, she thought.

Finally, after assuring Susan that if she needed anything at all she wouldn't hesitate to contact her, she closed the door of her upstairs room and breathed deeply as she looked around. It was pleasantly furnished in pastels with full-length windows on two sides that opened on to a veranda. From the veranda, she realised she was indeed just above the beach and had a lovely view, and that Ricky Emerson's room next door faced the same way and his veranda was separated from hers by a wooden latticework screen. But there was no sign of life on his veranda or sound from his room, and Evonne moved inside again, glanced at the wide smooth bed and decided she was not so much hungry now as sleepy, so she opened a bag and withdrew a filmy sarong, stripped and wrapped herself in it and lay down. Two minutes later she was asleep.

It was four o'clock before she woke, and the sun was starting to slide towards the horizon. She stood just inside the glass veranda door and gazed around for a couple of minutes. The beach looked incredibly inviting and the bay was studded with the colourful sails of little catamarans skimming the water. A swim, she thought, will just about complete the cure. Then I'll be ready to take on the world as well as Ricky Emerson.

Her costume was one-piece and strapless, emerald and black, emerald to her hips, utterly figure-hugging with a turnover stitched cuff across her breasts, and briefly black below. She tied her hair back with a black gabardine ribbon, searched briefly through her case for the thick emerald beach towel she had brought, picked up her sunglasses with the green frames and sallied forth.

She found herself a long white lounger on the beach which was not crowded but not deserted either, draped her towel on it and stood for a moment contemplating the water. Because they were inside the Great Barrier Reef, there was no surf, just a gentle lapping against the pale golden sand, and because the tide was high all available modes of water transport were in use. People were not only sailing the catamarans but paddling surf skis, riding sailboards and windsurfers and queueing up to water-ski—there was obviously only one place to be on this beautiful summer afternoon, in or on the water. Evonne contemplated no longer.

She was not a strong swimmer, but she stayed in for over half and hour, so safe was the water, so refreshing and with such a beautiful clean sandy bottom.

And when she finally came out, she decided Captain Cook and Matthew Flinders had definitely missed out on a small bit of paradise!

It was a low whistle that brought her back to earth as she came to her lounger and picked up her towel. A wolf whistle, for all that it had been barely audible, and for some reason it didn't occur to her that it was directed *at* her until she turned around and found herself looking straight into a pair of lazy green eyes beneath a ragged straw hat. Then there could be no doubt as that same green gaze travelled over her from head to toe in an insolently admiring manner, and a rather wry smile twisted a pair of chiselled lips as she froze for a moment with her towel bunched up in her hands.

In the next moment, however, she was mentally castigating herself for this breach in her usually iron-clad defences, and employing a tactic she occasionally fell back on. She stared back coolly and observed that those lazy green eyes accompanied a rather splendid male physique sprawled out on a lounger and clad only in a pair of brightly hued cotton shorts. Over six foot, she judged, and tanned golden with wide, sleek shoulders, narrow hips and long legs on which the hairs were lighter gold. About thirty, she judged, her eyes travelling back to his face—what

she could see of it beneath the hat, and good-
looking even without those startlingly green eyes.
And above all, very sure of himself.

But then so am I, she reminded herself, and
unhurriedly turned away, gathered her sunglasses from the chair and walked away to
another free lounger, but one that put some distance of beach between them. She wasn't sure if
it was her imagination, but she thought she heard
the sound of low laughter following her, and for
another moment she reacted uncharacteristi-
cally—she felt her blood boil briefly and set her
teeth annoyedly. She even muttered beneath her
breath, 'Damn *men*!' before taking hold and
relaxing.

Her ploy appeared to work, though. Twenty
minutes later, when she glanced up the beach,
her insolent admirer had his back to her and was
surrounded by a bevy of girls—well, three, but
all young and gorgeous even from a distance and
obviously lapping up his company.

A glint of contempt lit Evonne's dark eyes
briefly, then she lay back and let the late afternoon sunlight caress and soothe her.

While she was showering and thinking rather
longingly of dinner, someone knocked loudly on
her door.

'Hell!' she muttered, stepping out and dabbing
at herself hastily with a towel, then awkwardly
donning a long watermelon-pink cotton robe,
'that must be Ricky! I'm coming,' she called as
the knock sounded again, definitely an impatient tattoo this time. 'I'm coming!' I just hope

you're not a little monster, she added to herself, fiddling for the sash, not finding it and, impatient herself now, wrapping the robe around her.

But it was no *little* monster standing outside the door with his hand raised to knock again. It was a tall man instantly recognisable even without his hat, for his green eyes, his body still only clad in shorts and despite the fact that he was leaning on a walking-stick.

'Oh, now look here,' said Evonne after a second during which her heart had beat an odd tattoo of its own, 'this is . . .'

'Good heavens!' the man broke in, amusement crinkling the corners of his eyes. 'Don't tell me *you're* Patterson?'

Evonne's mouth fell open.

'Uncle Amos sent me this ambiguous telegram this morning. He . . . er . . . neglected to mention that you were a woman.'

CHAPTER TWO

EVONNE fell back a pace, her lips still parted, her dark eyes stunned and uncomprehending.

'You are . . . this Patterson person Uncle Amos has seen fit to foist on to me?' Richard Carlisle Emerson enquired with a faint frown between his eyes. 'I bumped into Susan a few minutes ago and she said they'd put you next door.'

Evonne closed her mouth and licked her lips. 'I don't understand,' she said hoarsely. 'He said you were young—little more than a boy.'

The frown faded, to be replaced by a look of wry humour. 'Did he say that? I'm thirty-one— I guess he's well into his sixties now, Uncle Amos, so thirty could be little more than a boy to him...'

'No,' Evonne broke in raggedly. 'He even talked about the generation gap there would be between *me* . . . and you. There must be some mistake!'

'Perhaps there is a generation gap between us,' Richard Emerson countered. 'I'm pretty young at heart, whereas you look to me to be one sophisticated but rather uptight lady—also very beautiful,' he added softly, those green eyes roaming leisurely over her again.

'Oh!' She turned away in disgust and he took the opportunity to follow her into the room and close the door, and when she turned around he was standing behind her.

'I bet it's a long time since anyone called you Ricky,' she said bitterly.

'Well, yes, it's mostly Rick nowadays—why are you so upset about this?'

'Because your uncle Amos deliberately misled me, for reasons I've yet to fathom,' Evonne replied tautly.

'For that matter, me too,' Richard Emerson said meditatively. 'In fact I'm just as much in the dark as you. You see, his telegram, which I can show you—no, I can't, I threw it away in disgust—but believe me, it said...Patterson comma my very own personal assistant comma arriving today to take care of all your needs. Place yourself in these wise hands...Full stop. Whereupon I immediately perceived, or thought I did, the old lure with a different bait.'

Evonne stared at him.

'My uncle Amos,' he explained with a grin, 'has been trying to get me into his business for years. I thought this was a fresh approach, a different line...ah!' He looked at her searchingly. 'Was I right?'

Evonne compressed her lips.

'Then you are his personal assistant? And you have come to help me with my book and at the same time try to entice me into the world of haberdashery and hosiery, homeware and horticultural products...' He broke off and burst out laughing, then sobered and said with mocking respect, 'Uncle Amos, I salute you this time, I really do! This ploy is a stroke of pure genius—a real live, eminently desirable woman to take care of all my needs and woo...even seduce me into the business. The old boy might have even come up trumps this time!'

'If you've quite finished,' Evonne said icily but with a faint delicate flush staining her throat that he noticed and watched with idle fascination for a moment, 'I'd like to say a few words. *I* was lured into this...*ploy*,' she paused and stared him straight in the eye, 'under false pretences and therefore will have no qualms about ending my part in it at the earliest opportunity.'

He started to smile, but restrained himself and said gravely, 'Now, Patterson, that's a bit extreme, surely? Can't we discuss it further?'

'There's nothing to discuss.'

'All right, what if I admit I might have interpreted my uncle's colourful way with words a little...liberally?'

'There would still be nothing to discuss!'

'Just say I *were* little more than a boy, would you stay then? Is that your main grievance?'

'That,' said Evonne, unwisely, she was to realise later, 'and the fact that you obviously have no intention of gratifying your uncle—and aunt's—dearest wish. It would only be a waste of my time.'

'What about my book?' he demanded. 'I can assure you I desperately need your wise—although I would have thought exquisite would be a better description——' he corrected with a swift, downward glance '—hands for that.' He couldn't restrain his smile this time and the reminiscent little gleam that came to his green eyes as he said softly, 'I really wish now that I'd preserved that telegram.'

'*Mr* Emerson,' Evonne said grimly, and noted but did not understand the faint look of surprise, then speculation, that came to his green eyes, 'nothing on earth would induce me to have anything further to do with you!'

He was silent for a time as he observed her curiously and until Evonne became uncomfortably aware of how lightly she was clad. Then he said softly, 'Because I whistled at you?'

She looked at him disdainfully and as if that was the last thing in the world she would care about, as if it was totally beneath her notice.

He smiled slightly. 'Because I laughed, then? Tell me something, are you off men, Patterson?'

'Why should you assume that?'

'Your magnificent scorn,' he said barely audibly. 'Also the fact that you don't mind boys, apparently. Is that for your own peace of mind?'

'My peace of mind has nothing to do with you,' she retorted.

'Oh, but it does, Patterson,' he drawled. 'Because you see, for whatever purpose my uncle sent you to me, I intend to keep you.'

'*Don't* keep calling me that, and...'

'I don't know what else to call you. Are you a Miss or a Ms? I see you're not a Mrs, I saw that straight off—at least, at present you're not. Like to tell me about it?'

Evonne took a distraught breath, then counted to ten, marvelling at the same time at how she had contrived to let this encounter get so out of hand, and she shot Richard Emerson a fiery dark glance before she veiled her eyes and said with an effort, but coolly, 'I'm a Miss, I've never been married and my name is Evonne—and before you laugh, I do know about the emu here, my namesake, apparently. One or two other things I might enlighten you about—I'm very hungry because I missed lunch, no one has yet been able to keep me *anywhere* I don't want to be, and, while there are some men I like a lot, your brand of wolf-whistling insolence appears to me to be simply a mark of immaturity.'

But she might as well not have wasted her breath, because Richard Emerson placed his hand on his heart and sighed plaintively, 'I am undone.'

Evonne realised she was breathing heavily with frustration and futility.

'One thing I can rectify,' he added. 'I can take you to dinner. Perhaps you'll see things in a better light after you've eaten? Personally, I'm always impossible too, when I'm starving. I shall come back to collect you in, say—half an hour?' And he limped out, leaving Evonne staring after him, struck speechless.

One of the new outfits she had brought comprised a sleeveless, V-neck, crossover button-through top, over a slim skirt. It was also pillar-box red with narrow black stripes forming squares, but despite the colour, the material was silky and cool. Evonne put it on, adjusted the black patent belt at her waist, bloused out the top above the belt and smoothed it over her hips below, then slid her bare feet into black patent open-toed shoes with little heels. Then she paused in front of the bathroom mirror and studied her make-up and hair. In fact she wore not much make-up at all because of the heat, but her lips were painted to match the outfit, there was a delicate application of silvery grey eye-shadow on her eyelids beneath her naturally curved eyebrows that she didn't have to do much to at all, other than smooth with her fingertips. Her hair, which when loose was shoulder-length, she had brushed back from her face and put up in an elegant bun. It was an austere frame for her face but made her large dark eyes, fringed by long lashes that she had no need to augment, appear even larger.

She couldn't help but know that she possessed the kind of stunning looks that turned heads wherever she went, but there had been times when she would gladly have traded them for something else, something more subtle.

Perhaps, she mused as she stared at herself, that's why Richard Carlisle Emerson got under my skin so thoroughly. I really do detest being whistled at and treated to lecherous looks from perfectly strange men. It's degrading, and I don't think one has to be a militant feminist to think so. Incidentally, Evonne, what are you going to do about him? How will Amos react if you walk out on his nephew? I mean, I wouldn't really care normally, but ... She sighed and realised she wouldn't like to hurt her boss's feelings. Then a frown creased her brow and her thoughts took another, though related, tack. Had Amos deliberately misled her into thinking his nephew was barely out of his teens? Or—well, yes, she acknowledged to herself, you've known Amos long enough to know that beneath that shrewd brain, the vision and all the rest of it, he can be oddly naïve and . . . I don't know what the right word for it is, but the kind of thing that makes a man who's made a fortune wear his wife's hand-knitted jumpers and wear them with pride even though she gets the pattern a little mixed up at times. Does that same fond blindness genuinely extend to his nephew? I suppose it's just possible it could . . .

Richard Emerson's unmistakable knock sounded on her door again, breaking into her thoughts and causing her expression to become so severe that she startled herself and had to smile ruefully and admonish herself, That's not the way to play it at all, Evonne. Take care!

She took her time about putting on her watch and the slim gold bangle she always wore before she answered the door.

His reaction as she opened the door was pre-dictable—at first. He pursed his lips to whistle softly, but stopped himself with a wry grimace and an odd glint in his green eyes. 'Dear me,' he drawled, 'you could be right, Patterson. There must be an enormous generation gap between us—*something* about you has to be responsible for these boyish outbursts you keep provoking in me!'

But Evonne had herself well in hand. 'If you've just spent a year studying the Kukukukus—if that part of the story is correct, at least, any female who doesn't wear a bone through her nose would probably appeal to you.'

He laughed with a flash of white teeth and for a second the impact, the golden impact of his tanned skin, sun-bleached hair and the startling contrast of his green eyes, together with his intensely alive, carefree, quizzical yet curious, clever but laid-back aura, took Evonne's breath away. In the instant that followed, she discovered to her amazement that she felt about a hundred years old, then she realised that he was staring at her with his laughter fading.

'What's wrong?' he queried.

'Nothing,' she said hastily—too hastily.

'You looked—for a moment you looked...' He shrugged, but his eyes were alert and intent as they lingered on her face.

She suppressed a curious shiver, like a warning bell striking at her nerves but warning her of what? 'I really am very hungry,' she explained.

'My apologies, ma'am! Do you mind if I lead the way?'

'Not at all,' she said politely.

The restaurant was upstairs on the second and top floor of the long building that housed several lounges and bars as well as the island shop. It had a broad veranda also set with tables and chairs and faced the beach and water. The last lingering light of the sunset was laying a metallic sheen on the sea as they took their seats at a table for two next to the full-length glass front walls of the restaurant.

Evonne looked around, then back at her companion, and was vaguely relieved to feel normal and in command of herself. Why she should have felt otherwise she couldn't imagine, but here, amid the subdued chatter of other diners, amid the soft chinking of glassware and cutlery, the background music, the dim light, the aroma of food, even Richard Carlisle Emerson looked as if he could be coped with.

A faint smile curved her lips as she studied him and recalled her mental image of him. Short-sighted and earnest he was not. Damp-palmed? Well, she doubted it—all the opposite, in fact, in his casual, loose-fitting white shirt with two big pockets that were all the rage, his stone-washed grey jeans, his streaked hair falling across his brow... I've dealt with hundreds of the likes of him, haven't I? she reflected.

'May I share the joke?'

'You may,' she said promptly, and told him what his uncle's description of him had conjured up in her mind's eye.

He looked amused. 'No wonder I came as a bit of a surprise! I gather either the imminent prospect of food or the half-hour of reflection you had while you dressed has seen some changes to your earlier mood of extreme militancy?'

It was some time before Evonne got the chance to reply, as the waitress descended on them and they ordered their meal and a bottle of wine of Richard's choice. Then Susan stopped at the table with details of the night's entertainment, which was to take the form of a talent contest, and the news that interested parties were being asked to form groups to either sing, dance or whatever took their fancy.

'Susie, no,' Richard said laughingly. 'I do not intend to expose myself that way.'

'But, Rick, just about everyone I've spoken to wants you to join their group. You're the most sought-after person here tonight—you sing, you're a mimic—you can even dance with a walking-stick. Please, Rick!' she pleaded.

'Don't mind me,' murmured Evonne.

'Would *you* care to be involved in this madness?' Rick enquired of her.

'No,' Evonne said definitely.

'Sorry, Susie,' he said promptly. 'It is Evonne's first night—perhaps tomorrow we'll join in whatever you've got planned.'

'Oh, all right,' said Susan with a grin. 'Just don't forget you're in the golf competition tomorrow. Can I put your name down for that, Evonne?'

Evonne hesitated.

'It doesn't matter if you're the most rank amateur—it's all a lot of fun, I promise you.'

Conscious of Rick's eyes on her and conscious that she had made the transition from thinking of him as young Ricky Emerson and then Richard Carlisle Emerson in capitals and now to Rick, which seemed to suit him eminently, she nodded at last. 'All right.'

'Great!' Susan wandered off in search of more victims.

'I thought these island resorts were supposed to be havens of peace,' Evonne remarked as her entrée was placed before her.

'You don't have to do a thing if you don't want to. Is that the type of person you are?'

'I'm not much good at sport, if *that's* what you mean. And I'm a lousy singer, hopeless as

a mimic, although I can... well, all in all I must
be that type of person,' she said ruefully.

'And yet you must be frightfully efficient—I
imagine being Uncle Amos's personal assistant
is a pretty high position, not to mention one that
frequently places you in the spotlight.'

Evonne finished her prawn cocktail. 'That's
different,' she said quietly.

'Which must mean there are two very different
Pattersons—the public and the private one.'

She dabbed her lips with her napkin, then
looked across at him. 'Probably.'

'I wonder,' Rick said slowly, 'how much I'll
ever get to know of the private one. By the way,
you haven't had a chance to comment on my
earlier supposition.'

She sipped her wine, then said evenly, 'Rick—
if I may call you that...'

'Be my guest. You could call me Emerson, then
I wouldn't feel so bad about calling you
Patterson, which just seems to spring to my lips.'

Evonne stared into his amused, oddly mocking
green eyes. 'I don't mind what you call me,' she
said, 'but if you want me to stay, it will have to
be on my terms.' She held his gaze deliberately.

'Go on,' he murmured.

'I promised your uncle I'd give you three weeks
of my time. I also promised him I would... test
the water concerning your future ambitions, but
you've made it quite clear there's no point, so,
if you do need help with your book, I'll confine
myself to that. But it will be a business arrangement, no more.'

'What made you change your mind?' he enquired after a long pause.

'I'm very fond of your uncle—and your aunt. He in particular has been very good to me. I don't care to hurt his feelings or go back on my word to him.'

'Are you saying your conception of me would hurt his feelings?'

'Yes,' Evonne said coolly.

A bright little flame sprang up in those green eyes, rendering them curiously tiger-like. 'You make some very snap judgements, Patterson.'

She shrugged and crumbled a roll between her fingers.

'You're not going to refute the charge?' he drawled.

'If you really want me to, I will, although I'll only be repeating myself. I'm curiously allergic to your type of man,' she said simply.

He laughed, but as if he was genuinely amused, which surprised Evonne a little as she recalled that tiger-like gleam in his eyes which seemed to have been doused and was only an elusive memory now. But of course he retaliated, as she knew he would. 'I just hope you don't live to regret these summary decisions, my dear,' he said lightly, still smiling slightly. 'So,' he added, 'now you've sorted that out, what are we left with?'

'If you'd like to show me your notes after dinner,' Evonne said tranquilly, 'I might get some idea of what's involved. Perhaps I should make one last point, though. There's a limit, fond as I am of your uncle Amos, to what I'll undergo on his behalf.'

'You know,' Rick said immediately, and topped up her wine, 'if you really are so allergic to masculine admiration, I'm surprised you haven't joined a nunnery, I really am.'

'I've thought...' She bit her lip.

'You've thought of it?'

'No, not really.'

'It doesn't surprise me. Not now that I know what one innocent wolf whistle has unleashed,' he marvelled. 'I tell you what, I'll think twice before I ever do it again. Are you sure the feminist movement hasn't employed you to go around the world crushing...'

It was the arrival of the main course that saved Evonne, in more ways than one. Because as he spoke, she had found herself thinking involuntarily that she might, just might have gone over the top. Why? she wondered, as she stared at the vegetables being dished on to her plate. And what on earth had made her admit that one half-formed and since wholly discarded idea that a nunnery might be the only place she could survive?

She tore her gaze from her plate, blinked and said at random, 'Sorry. But if you knew what it was like to be whistled at and... looked at in a certain way, and how *tired* you get of it... Perhaps I over-reacted. All the same...' She stopped a little helplessly and their gazes caught and held.

'Well now,' Rick said softly, 'that puts a different complexion on things.'

'It doesn't, you know,' she said. 'I mean, while I apologise for...'

'Swatting a fly with a concrete mixer?'

'Something like that,' she said ruefully, 'but all the same...'

'There's absolutely no future for me with you?' he proffered.

'No. Not...no.'

'Not *romantically*?'

'No.'

'One last question—are you some other man's sole domain, Patterson?'

For a second something protesting within her cried out, but she stilled it, and took refuge in silence, letting only her eyes speak for her in a dark, shuttered glance.

'All right,' he said abruptly, and surprised her by adding, 'eat your dinner, it's getting cold and you were starving, remember?'

After the remainder of their meal, during which he had made charming but entirely neutral conversation, Rick took her downstairs and bought her a liqueur in the lounge bar later to be used for the talent contest. There was a dance floor and stage and many comfortable cane chairs and tables from which to view the proceedings, but it was dim and quiet and deserted as they sipped their drinks at the bar.

'Not taking part tonight, Rick?' the barman queried in a friendly manner but with his eyes lingering on Evonne.

'No. I may come back and watch later, but tonight I'm going to let everyone else make fools of themselves,' said Rick with a grin.

'The old ankle playing up?'

'That's as good an excuse as any!'

'How is your ankle mending?' Evonne asked as the barman drifted away to serve a newcomer.

'Apart from the odd ache when I overdo things, it's pretty good.'

'How did you break it?'

'I ... er ... tripped.'

She raised an eyebrow. 'Down a vine-infested jungle pathway in the wilds of Papua?'

'Down a pathway,' he agreed, and his green eyes glinted wickedly.

'You might as well tell me,' she said.

'I don't think I ought to tell you at all—but then again, what have I got to lose? The damage has already been done. I was ... er ... attempting to make a hasty getaway from a house in Port Moresby where I'd been invited to ... er ... spend the night by this charming little Swiss lady who had assured me her boyfriend was many, many miles away, and that anyway he was such a boor, she really wanted to dump him and was in need of advice and ... consolation. I really,' he marvelled, 'can't believe my own naïveté!'

Evonne had to smile, which caused Rick to raise his eyebrows. 'You're not absolutely disgusted?' he asked quizzically.

'Tell me what happened.'

'Well, before any ... er ... real consolation could take place, the boyfriend turned up, and he turned out to be a massive Yugoslav in a very bad temper because he'd walked, flown and clawed his way from Ok-Tedi, which is this goldmine rather a long way away from Moresby, to spend the weekend with his beloved, to surprise her. What really surprised *me* and all but cost me my life was how the lady reacted. Her emotions did a complete about-face, she started to tear what little clothing she had left on to shreds, in an instant she reduced her hair-do, which had been a work of art, all golden and braided, to incredible disorder, and if all that wasn't bad enough, she proceeded to accuse me, in a voice that would have done a banshee credit, of trying to rape her. I had no choice but to leave rather hurriedly, via a window and then this tortuous path, which was extremely steep and...you're laughing,' he said reproachfully. 'Believe me, it was no laughing matter at the time.'

'I can imagine,' Evonne said unsteadily.

'You know something—you should laugh more. It's like...it's like moonlight shining on dark glossy water.' Rick stared at her, his eyes alert and curious.

Evonne sighed, but a smile still played on her lips. 'And I'm beginning to think you're incorrigible, you know,' she said mildly. 'Will you show me your notes now or should we leave it until tomorrow? I'm...actually I'm a bit tired. I don't know why,' she added with some surprise.

'Perhaps you're just human, after all,' he observed. 'And before you get your hackles up, I mean susceptible to leaving home at the crack of dawn and flying across a continent, susceptible to a rather radical change in climate—this humidity does take it out of you—like the rest of us mere mortals.'

'I'm really not surprised you're a writer, or trying to be,' she said tartly before she could stop herself. 'You're obviously intoxicated with words, but perhaps you should be an actor instead. Then you could really spout away to your heart's content.'

'Now that's not very nice,' he drawled, 'but I've noticed this rather surprising tendency you have before.'

Evonne closed her eyes wearily.

'This tendency,' he went on, not the least perturbed, 'you have of—how can I put it?—of allowing the sophistication and containment and *maturity* you wear, like a beautiful curtain almost, to fall aside very fleetingly to reveal just a glimpse of...claws and a rather street-wise toughness,' he said with a considering frown.

Evonne compressed her lips and tried to contain her response, but again without success. 'I am tough and street-wise, Mr Emerson,' she said coldly. 'Like your bad-tempered Yugoslav, I've also clawed my way up.'

'That's very interesting,' Rick said quietly, his green eyes never leaving her face.

She made a futile sound and stood up. 'I'm going to bed,' she said curtly.

'I'll walk you there.' He stood up.

'That's not necessary...'

'Yes, it is, you could run into anything out there.'

'You must be joking!' she said incredulously, and turned on her heel.

But he was not, and he followed her out but at a little distance after signing for the drinks, so that she was half-way down the path towards their block ahead of him, when something ghostly and black and feathery, thin and sinuous of neck and with a malevolent eye, appeared out of the darkness beside her and made a noise she could only afterwards describe as a petrifying whoomp of sound.

She jumped, gasped and fell back with her heart racing madly and her mouth going dry as the thing advanced on her.

'It's all right,' Rick Emerson said from right behind her. 'It's only your namesake.'

'My...' Her lips trembled. 'Oh, lord, the *emu*!'

'Mmm. She's really quite harmless. Look.' And he proceeded to scratch the bird's neck, which caress was accepted with another, this time deeply gratified, whoomp.

'Oh,' Evonne said weakly. 'What else lurks around here at night?'

'Kangaroos,' he replied promptly, and took her hand as Yvonne wandered off. 'They're generally shyer than Yvonne, but they do roam around all over the island. It's quite a sight to see them feeding on the golf course after dark—you can see them by the tennis court floodlights. Would you like to wander down to have a look now?'

'I...'

'You're still shaking,' he said.

'I feel very foolish,' she admitted ruefully. 'Perhaps another night. You've left your walking-stick behind.'

'Damn—if I lose that one it'll be about the sixth, but it's quite safe...'

'You'd better go and get it,' she interrupted. 'Who knows what could happen to it during a talent contest? I'll be fine now and I'm really as tired as any mere mortal. Goodnight.' She withdrew her hand and walked away.

Rick watched her go, but didn't follow, nor did she see that he stood in the path for several minutes after she was out of sight before turning and limping back to the lounge.

But to end a thoroughly contrary day, once upstairs in the privacy and safety of her room Evonne found she wasn't sleepy-tired any more—mind-weary, certainly, but also oddly keyed up.

She changed into an oyster satin short nightgown with shoestring straps and intricate lace and appliqué panels, but took it off almost immediately and found a plain blue cotton one with no appliqué or lace or see-through panels. Then she removed her make-up and brushed her hair—and wondered what the hell the matter was and why she felt thoroughly jumpy and on edge.

'Surely one man ... of the type you've *never* been attracted to ... hasn't done this to you?' she asked herself, standing before the built-in dressing-table mirror studying her naked face and loose hair. 'Well, he's certainly provoked you successfully a couple of times, he's even dug out some things you thought you'd successfully submerged years ago, but what would he know about being tough and street-wise? He's probably led a charmed life from day one, what with a diplomat for a father—he sounds well-educated and he appears to have the wherewithal to do crazy thinks like indulge in a year of amateur anthropology stroke archaeology. Something of a typically good-looking dilettante, if you ask me...'

She stopped abruptly and stared at herself even harder because she thought she could detect something oddly shrewish in her expression. 'Oh, Evonne,' she whispered, 'you always could be a shrew sometimes. Especially when you were on the defensive, which you were so often—but why now? You've got to the top of the tree...'

I must be very tired, she thought, turning away from her disturbing presence in the mirror. And still thinking about...will I ever forget? What if I hadn't been able to come away from the Anniversary Dinner? What if I hadn't been able to feign some temporary disease, what if I ever just bump into Rob and Clarry one day, what if a terrible sense of curiosity takes me back for it, just to see how they are? No, no...I wouldn't do that to myself, and that's why I'll stay here and beat Richard Carlisle Emerson at his own game!

'And it's just occurred to me how to do that,' she mused, with a sudden, almost hysterical little jolt of laughter. 'I'll treat you as if you were young Ricky Emerson. I'll be just like your maiden aunt!'

CHAPTER THREE

'ARE these they?'

'That's them,' Rick Emerson said. 'My life's work, my contribution to society, my wit, my perception, my scientific knowledge—some of it, my excellent grammar—my notes in other words, my precious though fragmented masterpiece.'

'And you couldn't find anything more suitable for your fragmented ... manuscript than a series of old brown paper grocery bags?' Evonne enquired as she studied the pile he had just dumped on her bed.

'An artist uses whatever material happens to be at hand.'

'I'll take your word for it,' she said wryly.

'You're very calm this morning, Patterson,' Rick Emerson commented, calmly draping his tall golden frame on her bed alongside the paper bags, crossing his arms behind his head and staring up at her thoughtfully. He again wore only his multi-coloured shorts.

'What do you think you're doing?' she said tartly.

'My ankle's sore. I'm resting it. We've just played five holes of competition golf, if you recall.'

'I recall,' said Evonne. 'Remind me not ever to believe you when you say you're also only an amateur at anything.'

He grinned. 'I am!'

'Then I must be the most useless person who ever held a golf club.'

'I wouldn't say that. Just to watch you walking along, swinging it, was a source of great inspiration to me—and not a few others, before you take umbrage. There's something about your figure in shorts that's quite electrifying.'

Evonne glanced down at her fashionably long, slate-grey thin linen shorts and white sleeveless scoop-necked blouse which was now sticking to her and damp in patches—and remembered her plan. 'Flattery will get you nowhere, Rick. Tell me, does this book have any...form?'

He sat up with a frown. 'What do you mean? Of course it does!'

'I mean like a beginning, a middle and an end. Or is it a series of...sequences? And before *you* take umbrage,' she continued serenely, to his definite look of annoyance, 'I'm only asking because I just don't know what to expect.'

'This book,' he said precisely, 'is in journal form—diary form, if you like. From the day I decided to go to Papua New Guinea to the day I left. It takes the *form* of all my experiences, anecdotal as well as the scientific observations I made...'

'What about your experiences of the Swiss/ Yugoslav persuasion?' Evonne put in innocently.

For once, Rick hesitated, but not for long. 'Some,' he admitted, 'but nothing to get your puritan knickers in a knot about, Patterson. I've only actually detailed my failures, not my...'

'Victories?' she supplied.

'I don't sleep and tell,' he said virtuously.

'I'm relieved to hear you say so,' she replied, and favoured him with the closest she could come to whatever the feminine version of an avuncular smile was called.

He narrowed his green eyes immediately. 'Have I missed something somewhere along the line?'

'Missed? I doubt if you miss much at all . . . so, is it all dated and in order, then?' Evonne gestured at the paper bags, then frowned doubtfully. 'There seems to be an awful lot of it.'

'It's in perfect order, although once it's legible it might need some editing.'

'Legible?' she queried warily. 'It's not in Pidgin—whatever?'

Rick laughed. 'No, it's not.'

'Then . . . ?' She stared at him.

'Didn't Uncle Amos tell you? He always says I should have been a doctor, I have this . . .'

'Oh, no!' Evonne muttered, and leant across him to pick up a bag and extract a piece of foolscap from it, covered in a large round writing that resembled hieroglyphics to her despite its sprawling size. She groaned. 'Why me, and how did you ever learn to write like this?'

'My mother claims it's because no one realised I was left-handed and was originally taught to write with my right. In fact I have all sorts of odd personality quirks because of that. I trip, I lose things . . .'

'And talk a lot of nonsense,' Evonne said wearily. 'This could take me months! I didn't realise I would have to type out a whole manuscript which I can't read in the first place, I thought you needed someone to help you edit it and perhaps type up some amendments. Why didn't *you* type it in the first place?' she demanded. 'You must know no one can read your writing!'

'I can't type,' he said meekly. 'I've tried, but my left-handed syndrome doesn't allow it. Also, when you're crawling through a crocodile-infested swamp and you come to a bit of high dry ground, it's much simpler to take out some paper and a pencil, which I always kept in a waterproof wallet upon my person, and record things there and then, rather than waiting until you can lay your hands on a typewriter or carry one around with you.'

Evonne let the sheet of foolscap flutter to the bed. 'I don't believe you,' she said. 'I don't think I believe one word you say. You make it up as you go along, don't you?'

Rick's eyes sparkled with laughter, but he said gravely, 'I've certainly crawled through a crocodile-infested swamp.'

'And I've...' Evonne bit her lip and turned away, only to tense as Rick said gaily and got up lithely, 'Relax, Patterson! Uncle Amos obviously has great faith in you. So have I. Once you master my handwriting—and I'll be here to help you every step of the way—it will be a piece of cake.'

'No, it *won't*,' she said intensely, and sank down into a cane armchair with her face in her hands.

'Evonne,' he said after a time, and when she looked up at last he seemed to have changed character. The lines and angles of his face were set differently; for once his green eyes were not amused or mocking but narrowed and oddly determined, even carrying a faint look of hauteur, and she realised she had dimly been aware of this capacity he had of stepping into another skin, rather like the curtain he had accused her of lifting, aware that beneath the charm and the humour there lurked a tiger... She blinked at herself impatiently and said dully, 'What?'

'I'm rarely serious about anything, but there are one or two things I take to heart. If I start a project, I always see it through and I do it well. This book is no exception to that rule, whatever you and Uncle Amos may have decided to the contrary.'

'It's not that I mean to belittle your book,' said Evonne, and flushed slightly.

'No?' His eyes taunted her. 'Be that as it may, when I idly happened to mention to my beloved uncle that I needed some help on it, it wasn't *my* idea that he send me his very own personal assistant who would have her nose put out of joint—all I said I needed was a typist, some patient soul who wouldn't mind deciphering my handwriting. *He* then said, "I've got just the person for you, someone with journalistic experience who was once even Robert Randall's Press secretary!"'

Evonne winced inwardly.

Rick went on, 'Then his telegram arrived and I smelt a rat but also thought—why's he sending me a bloke? They're not as a rule great typists, and do I need somebody's ex-Press secretary to make suggestions and generally irritate the life out of me?'

'What, I hesitate to ask, did you answer yourself?' Evonne enquired with some return of spirit.

'Because of the time I wasted on this infernal ankle, I'm behind schedule, my dear Patterson, so I thought I'd wait and see what transpired. After all, why knock back a pig's ear before you've had a chance of assessing its capability for being a silk purse instead?' A glimmer of a smile disturbed his expression for the first time. 'I've never before had the opportunity to use that expression so aptly,' he mused.

'I'm surprised, but...'

'Let me finish,' he commanded. 'At least let's sort the wheat from Uncle Amos's chaff—are you a good typist?'

'Yes, but...'

'Do you have a journalistic background?'

'I did a course...'

'I mean practically? *Were* you Robert Randall's Press secretary, and how did you get that job?'

Evonne took a breath. 'Yes, I was,' she said steadily. 'And I worked my way up through advertising copywriting, magazine editing, a stint in a publishing house and some time in the business section of a daily paper, but...'

He had been leaning back against a wall with his arms folded, his legs crossed so that his bad ankle was resting on his good one, but he straightened swiftly and came to stand over her. 'Then you're bloody perfect for this job, Patterson!'

Evonne stared up at him dazedly. 'You just said—rather, about two hundred words ago you *said* the last thing you needed...*all* you needed was a sweet-tempered typist...'

'I need a good, happy, interested typist, and coming from you, I wouldn't even mind some suggestions. Truly! But what I meant, later, was that *you* could find it really interesting. I mean, one way or another it's your career, but this might be a delightfully different branch of it. You might even be inspired to write a book yourself. Most people who take up journalism dream of doing that, don't they?'

'I...' She closed her eyes.

'Is something pulling you back to Melbourne? Something that's making you spurn the chance of a wonderful, different holiday, an experience? Like a couple of kids, despite your being a Miss and never married?'

'*No!*'

'It happens.'

'Not to me.' To her horror, Evonne felt tears on her lashes and she stood up abruptly and dashed at them. 'I...'

Rick caught her wrist and swung her round to face him. 'But there's something...rather unhappy down there, isn't there?' he said very quietly.

'No.'

'Something that's put you off balance. I can see it in your eyes. This morning you started out treating me as if I was ten—from the moment you laid eyes on me, you've been disturbed,

angry, at odds—unless I remind you acutely of
some lost or perfidious lover...?' He waited.

'You don't.'

'Then something's happened to make the world
go dark for you. I can't believe you've got where
you are if you're as thin-skinned and unsure of
yourself as you appear to be.'

They were very close and he still had his fingers
linked round her wrist—so close she had to tilt
her head back slightly to look into his eyes, and
the dark depths of hers were a little stunned, wary
and disbelieving that this man who had only
known her for not yet twenty-four hours could
read her like this.

Her throat worked and for an instant a fleeting
sense of being stranded caught at her nerves—to
go back was madness, to stay... but what could
be so dangerous about staying? She was no girl
to be seduced by a handsome face, by a pair of
broad golden shoulders, by a man who sometimes seemed younger than she was, by an insolent, boyish charm... What am I thinking? she
marvelled. I *am* probably more piqued than I realised, at being seconded to do a job any girl from
the typing pool could do. As for him...the
sudden memory of his tiger look as he had talked
about his book came to her...as for him, he needs
a typist, obviously, and he's the kind of person
who'll flatter and whatever to get his needs attended to. If only he didn't make me feel...I
don't know...vulnerable now.

'Well?' he said softly.

'It seems to me,' her voice was husky, 'I might
need a holiday after all. They say a change is as

good as one, don't they? And I can't quibble with the setting. If you really want me to stay, I will.'

Rick was silent and he watched her carefully for a long moment before he said, 'You wouldn't also like to confide in me, would you?'

'No—at least,' her hand clenched involuntarily and he felt it through her wrist and his eyes narrowed as she went on with an effort, 'there's nothing except that I probably am thin-skinned and not the most patient person in the world. I could arrange for someone else for you, though.'

He released her wrist, stepped back and said with a curiously twisted smile, 'We'll muddle through somehow, Patterson. Why don't you put those gorgeous togs on and come for a swim?'

Evonne started to frown and opened her mouth, but she shut it and after a moment nodded.

'That's my girl!' he drawled. 'I'll go down and commandeer a couple of loungers for us.'

That afternoon, however, she became businesslike.

She requested of the housekeeper, and got, a table and straight-backed chair, she resolutely shut out the view and adjusted the air-conditioning so that she could work in comfort with the windows closed and disturb no one at the same time. She typed out—the quick brown fox jumps over the lazy dog, and, half a page lower—Mary had a little lamb, its fleece was white as snow, and everywhere that Mary went, the lamb was sure to go.

She took the piece of paper in to Rick next door and handed it to him with a pen. 'Write that out, will you, underneath the typing?'

He scanned the sheet. 'What the devil for...oh, I see. This is going to be your guide. Not a bad idea, Patterson, but we can go over a few pages together and...'

'No,' Evonne said firmly, 'I'm best off trying to master it alone, which I expect to have done by this evening. Then I'll get you to check what I've typed.'

'Well—but look here, I don't expect you to work yourself to death or your fingers to the bone...'

'I don't intend to,' she interrupted, 'but I plan to work a part of each day, and at that rate it should be done within a week.'

'Should it, now?' he said with a grin. 'It doesn't have to be, you know. I have a fortnight before I'm due to present it to my editor.'

'You have an editor?'

'Of course. You sound surprised.'

'I...' Evonne hesitated. 'I...'

Rick waited with one eyebrow raised, then said deliberately, 'I don't know why people take this unprofessional view of me—some people. When I got the idea of spending my sabbatical the way I did, and writing a book, I naturally approached a publisher first to discuss its viability and whether they'd be interested. I approached several and one, a university press, indicated that they would...surely that's the *professional* way to go about things?'

'Oh, it is,' Evonne said hastily. 'My apologies. I...er...' She broke off and glanced around at the colourful chaos of his room. 'Perhaps it's because you don't seem to be a terribly...organised sort of person that one gets these false impressions—don't you ever hang any of your clothes up?'

'Not often,' he replied. 'And do you know why?'

'Your left-handed syndrome?' she hazarded.

'Well,' he shrugged, 'that too, probably, but in hotels and resorts I do it as a form of protest. I resent the fact that they automatically assume I'm going to pinch their hangers and have installed the horribly ingenious new kind without hooks that you have to slot into permanent rings on the rails.'

Evonne stared at him, at the genuine hauteur of his expression, and said feebly, 'You are a bit mad, you know,' then dissolved into helpless laughter.

'Don't tell me you've never grappled with them and found them fiddly and irritating!'

'Yes, you're right, I have.'

'Then why don't you join me in my protest?'

'Because I have too much respect for my clothes. Will you please write that out and let me get to work?'

'You say that as if it's downright dangerous to stay in my company any longer.' He looked offended.

'I think it probably could be. It might be catching,' she said gaily and with no presentiment at all of the kind of prediction she had made. And she accepted the piece of paper after he had written on it with a grave thank you and a murmured, 'Like General MacArthur, I shall return, later.'

Nor did she even stop to query, as she let herself back into her room, why she should be feeling curiously light-hearted and unburdened, let alone not even daunted by the task she had undertaken. In fact it took quite a few days for the implications to sink in...

Over the next couple of days, Evonne worked exactly as she'd said she would. It was slow work at first until she became accustomed to Rick's impossible writing, but gradually she got used to it, and several things happened.

She became both enchanted and puzzled. She became conversant with some unusual statistics—for example, that the population of Papua New Guinea, which represented point ten per cent of the world's population, spoke fifteen per cent of the world's languages—hundreds of them, and some spoken only by a few hundred people. She learnt about upland basins in the highlands, the great river systems such as the Fly and the Sepik, the Bulolo region where gold had first been discovered. She learnt about the Ok-Tedi mine on the headwaters of the Fly, but it was when she started on the third chapter of Rick Emerson's book—it was divided into chapters, although it was in journal form—that the enchantment came through loud and clear—also the puzzlement. The third chapter was entitled, 'Bilong wonem yu faitim dispela plisboi?'—with two translations below. 'Belong what name you fight 'im dis fellow police boy?' and 'Why did you hit this policeman?'

The entries that followed were all about Rick's often hilarious encounters with Pidgin before he felt he had mastered it—only to discover time and time again that he never might.

Evonne voiced her puzzlement that night over dinner.

It was extremely hot, and she had put her hair up and put on a simple white cotton halter-neck dress.

'Rick, what exactly are you?' she asked as she broke a roll and reached for the butter.

He looked wary. 'What do you mean?'

'What do you actually do? I mean—well, your book seems to be about a rather accident-prone statistician of some kind. I'm not knocking it,' she went on hastily. 'It's very funny and it has a curious charm that's quite...makes it quite compulsive reading, but...' She stopped and frowned. 'What science are you actually pursuing?'

'Oh, that,' he said with a grin. 'The mother of 'em all.'

'The...? I still don't understand.'

'Not surprising,' he commented. 'It's an enormous subject. I'm a geographer.'

Her surprise was clearly evident now.

He said with a wry twist of his lips, 'Did you think they'd become extinct?'

'No,' she said slowly, 'well...' And she made a helpless little gesture.

Rick sat forward with a gleam in his green eyes. 'This obviously calls for an explanation. Geography is the science that describes the earth's surface and, in consequence, everything on it and immediately above and below it that affects it. And because that's such a vast area it's become a science subject to a lot of fission.'

Evonne looked confused.

'How can I explain that?' he murmured to himself. 'Geography is the science that brings into a broad, overall picture what meteorologists, geologists, biologists, economists, demographers, political scientists, sociologists, historians—even psychologists, philosophers and theologians study separately. I'm out of breath!'

'I'm not surprised,' she said with a slight smile. 'It *sounds* exhausting. Wouldn't it be simpler to be say—just one or two of those others?'

'I've thought of that, but it's really the overall picture that intrigues me, although I do have a pet sort of specialisation of my own.'

'What's that?'

'Social and cultural geography. Which is,' he forestalled her, 'studying things like age-sex differences in populations, the changing patterns of language and religion in rural groups—that kind of thing.'

'Ah, now I'm beginning to see! But,' Evonne frowned, 'your observations don't seem to be terribly scientific, if you don't mind me saying so. You seemed to have had a lot of trouble keeping track of anybody, let alone of your possessions.'

'I always have that trouble with my possessions,' he said gravely, then looked at her with the light of sudden inspiration in his eyes. 'I obviously need someone like you to organise me, Patterson!'

'I suspect it could be an impossible task—you might need a wife.'

'Do you think so? I've got the feeling the last thing I could cope with is a wife, I'm sure I'd be very poor husband material.'

Evonne glanced at him through her lashes. 'Might you not just object to being pinned down in any way?'

'How wise you are, Patterson,' he said softly.

'Yes, well, to get back to your book...'

'Yes, well, perhaps we should shift to safer ground,' he drawled, and before she could take issue added, 'My book is actually only a sideline of the whole experience, a sort of tongue-in-cheek tilt at scientists who take themselves too seriously and a not too serious armchair guide for people who are vaguely interested in that kind of thing. My real studies, which are to be part of my thesis for a Doctorate, are much more scientific.'

'A Doctorate?' Evonne repeated, her eyes wide.

'You don't approve?'

'I...of course! I'm just trying to...your uncle,' she said disjointedly, 'didn't...'

Rick smiled affectionately. 'Uncle Amos, like so many people, has never been able to grasp what I do, never particularly *wanted* to either, but I understand that, he has his own axe to grind—what kind of disinformation did he pass on to you about my career?'

'He said he wasn't sure whether you were a budding anthropologist or archaeologist but that you seemed to be fascinated with the...er... intimate practices of the Kukukukus.'

Rick threw back his golden head and laughed delightedly. 'No *wonder* you were in a bit of a state when you arrived, Patterson! You were obviously expecting to be confronted by a sex-mad teenager!'

Evonne had to laugh a little herself. 'But I mean, what do you actually do for a living? Or don't you have to worry about that?'

For an instant his green eyes sparked, but almost immediately the spark was gone. 'I teach for a living,' he said mildly. 'At present at a Sydney university. And that's where I hope to complete my thesis.'

'Oh!'

'Now I've really floored you, by the sound of it.'

She looked rueful. 'Sorry. I'm just wondering if *anything* your uncle told me about you is true.'

'What else did he tell you?'

'That you father was a...an English diplomat and that you'd lived all over the world while you were growing up.'

'Now that *is* true. And probably why I regard the world as my oyster and have this fascination for it.'

'So,' Evonne said slowly, 'that's how you see yourself spending the rest of your life—as an academic and, really, an explorer of a kind.'

'I guess so,' he replied thoughtfully. 'Although it's probably foolish to make cast-iron predictions about those things, but I really can't see myself stepping into my uncle's shoes.'

'Why, then, does he persist in thinking you might?'

'I—actually, I rather thought he *had* accepted it lately, which just goes to show how wrong one can be.'

Evonne finished her meal in silence. Then she told him she was going back to work. He protested that she'd worked all afternoon, but she was unshakeable about it and he didn't persist.

In fact, she thought as she made her way back to her room, keeping a wary eye out for the emu, he's been very co-operative since I started to work on his book. He's been quite different. No more innuendoes, no more subtle or not so subtle looks, and pleasant company when we're together.

She thought about the time they had spent together that morning. The tide had been right for a very early sail, and when Rick had knocked on her door at what seemed like the crack of dawn to point this out to her, she'd blinked sleepily, then looked out of her windows, and immediately fallen prey to the vista of sea like pale blue shot silk.

'I don't know how to sail,' she'd said, though.

'I do. I'll teach you.'

'I don't know if I'm teachable, I'll be too scared...'

'Not with me, you won't,' he had assured her.

And later, on the beach, as one of the obliging beach boys had rigged up the sail for them, she had worried about the lack of wind. 'How can you sail without a breeze?'

'Patterson,' Rick had said patiently, 'trust me, will you? Once we get out a bit we'll pick a breeze.'

'But how do we get out?'

He had exchanged a wry look with the beach boy. 'We paddle if necessary. Will you just jump on and quit worrying!'

'I'll just do up my life-jacket properly...'

Rick had glanced heavenwards but restrained himself. Half an hour later, though, when the little craft was skimming the water before a playful breeze, when the world was still caught in a rose and gold early morning radiance, he had said teasingly, 'Should we take her in?'

'Oh, no—do we have to?'

'That's quite a reversal of how you felt earlier!'

'You've converted me,' Evonne had said enthusiastically. 'I had no idea it was so simple or such fun!' And she had laughed as he'd gybed the little craft expertly and a spray of sea-water had drenched her, a laugh of pure exhilaration.

He had been watching her and she'd thought for a moment he was going to say something admiring, but he hadn't, just offered to teach her more.

They'd come in and eaten an enormous breakfast, played a round of golf to work it off, then lazed on the beach until lunch. 'I'll be an all-rounder by the time I get back to Melbourne,'

Evonne had observed over lunch. 'Sailing, golf—all the social skills I lack.'

'I should have thought you have social skills in abundance,' Rick had said lazily.

'Oh, I can give a pretty good imitation of it,' she had answered lightly, then added, to allay the slight frown of curiosity she saw in his eyes, 'I'm only joking. What have you got on this afternoon?'

'I'm going fishing off the Deepwater Jetty—I don't suppose it's any good inviting you along?'

'No, thanks all the same.'

All the same, at five o'clock, when he hadn't returned, she had decided a walk down to the jetty was just what she needed. The path followed the railway line and, if one timed one's walk right, one could hitch a lift back on the train. She had been about half-way there, enjoying the smell of the thick, vine-festooned bush to one side as the ground rose quite steeply, and the beach and sea to her right with the water lapping gently amongst the rocks and coral, when she had heard the train coming towards her. It was more like a toy train, she had often thought, with its brightly coloured little engine and cars, but in fact it was a real workhorse—it was also extremely noisy, and she had jumped off the path, well out of its way, but turned to wave as was the custom on friendly Brampton.

Whereupon, with a screech of metal upon metal, it had pulled up and started to back towards her. Rick, she'd thought immediately, and had not been wrong. Rick had asked them to stop and pick her up, Rick had descended and handed her up, and she had become a part of the team of happy anglers and onlookers who made it something of a ritual to take a late afternoon walk to the Deepwater Jetty.

Rick, she thought, as she let herself into her room, who is so popular here with other guests and staff alike. He seems to draw people to him like a magnet. Does he always and has he always had that kind of happy personality that's never on the defensive, never prickly or always on the lookout for being patronised or snubbed?

'Like mine,' she murmured to herself with a grimace. 'I wonder what they think of me?'

It was obvious to her that there was some confusion, some speculation about their relationship. And because of the time she spent working, she realised, to some people her status was not quite fish, not quite fowl... or perhaps it's just my own peculiar brand of aloofness that makes them not quite sure how to treat me, she reflected. Then again, the occasional dark looks I get from all the nubile young ladies with which the place seems to abound are perfectly readable! If only they knew!

She came out of her reverie and went back to typing up—*Belong what name you fight 'im dis fellow police boy?*

Two more days passed.

Days in which her mind and body responded like a flower opening to the sun, she thought, and had to smile at her fancifulness. But she also had to admit that, if there was such a thing as island fever, she might have caught it. She cer-

tainly felt relaxed yet alive to the beauty around
her, soothed and sometimes almost sensually lazy
but as if her very pores were drinking in the sea,
the bush, the skies, the bird life, the incredibly
beautiful tropical fish and the coral in the narrow
channel between Brampton and Carlisle that
made snorkelling there like visiting a wonderland. And of course there was always Rick
Emerson's book to come back to, to amuse and
entertain her, even to find herself giggling like a
schoolgirl sometimes at his way of recounting his
experiences. If this doesn't become a best-seller,
she thought, I'll eat my hat.

So relaxed was she, she didn't even glimpse
what was waiting to pounce on her and tear it all
to shreds.

Six days after she came, they had their weekly
seafood dinner—a smörgasbörd, she was assured, of every seafood delicacy that flourished
in those waters: oysters, prawns, crabs, coral
trout—you name it, it would be there, plus lavish
salads . . . a veritable feast!

In honour of this veritable feast, Evonne put
on a chalk-blue shirred chiffon dress that clung
to her body, leaving her shoulders and arms bare,
and tucked some pink hibiscus blossoms into her
hair. Her pale skin now resembled warm ivory.

Rick had also dressed up in deference to this
dinner, in a cream denim battle jacket over his
open-necked beige shirt and pants, and as they
met outside their respective doors she studied him
critically, then said approvingly, 'You look very
nice.'

'Thank you, ma'am,' he replied with a wicked little grin. 'You, on the other hand, look so sensational you defy description.'

Her lips twitched. 'I think that's the first time I've known you to be lost for words,' she smiled.

'It's not that I am, really,' he countered immediately. 'I just don't want to offend you by getting...er...personal. However...'

'Rick, I believe you have to queue for this smörgasbörd. We don't want to be last, do we?'

He shot her an exasperated look. 'All right, I can take a hint. Lead on, Patterson, but if I were you I'd really be on the lookout for wolves tonight. The kind that whistle at you, I mean.'

Such was her state of serenity, Evonne smiled an almost dreamy little smile and said innocently, 'I believe you've even managed to set me straight on that issue. If it happens I'll ignore it outwardly and be inwardly flattered. What do you say to that?'

They were standing at the top of the steps, facing each other, and Rick inspected her upturned face and sparkling dark eyes, her lips painted to match the hibiscus twined into the night-darkness of her hair, and said, barely audibly, 'That's better.'

She raised her eyebrows. 'What is?'

'Nothing.' He took her hand. 'I've lost my stick. Care to help a recuperating cripple down these steps?'

'Not again!'

'It'll turn up. Anyway, I don't really think I need it any more.'

'Then you don't need my hand—there's also a railing,' she pointed out.

He lifted her hand to his lips and kissed it briefly, then released it, saying ruefully, 'That's my essential Patterson. Lead on—I'm starving!'

The seafood dinner was well worthy of its accolades.

'Mmm,' said Evonne, 'I doubt if I can even move after all that. It was superb.'

'They cater for that feeling too, on Seafood night,' Rick told her. 'There's a dance on down-stairs—starts slow, then hots up as the night wears on. You are coming, aren't you?'

She blinked. 'I . . .'

'Yes, you are,' he said determinedly. 'I'm not having you scuttling back to your typewriter tonight.'

'Well, I probably *should*. . .it's not going quite as fast as I thought it would, but. . .' She sat back with a sigh. 'No, I won't.'

Rick had opened his mouth, but he closed it, then said, 'I quite thought I was going to have to have a fight with you.'

'I don't seem to be so fightable these days, do I?' she observed, and stared into space until he asked her what she was thinking.

'I . . . don't know,' she confessed. 'Examining this new me, perhaps.' And for some reason she shivered as the first faint premonition stirred in her mind, but it wasn't even really decipherable at that stage, just an oddly elusive feeling of unease.

'Evonne...' He stopped as she smiled brilliantly at him.

'Yes?'

He hesitated, then shrugged. 'Let's go to this dance before you change your mind.'

I could have danced all night...

The refrain kept running through Evonne's mind as she danced a part of the night away—often with Rick until his ankle began to ache, then with anyone who happened to ask her, because it was one of those happy nights when everyone danced with everyone else and no one appeared to get jealous, and anyway, the staff handled it all very tactfully by running a small competition and making everyone change partners. A night when the music got into her soul and when her one social skill, as she thought of it, that seemed to have come to her naturally, outclassed nearly everyone else there.

'You're fantastic!' 'Do you dance for a living?' 'Where have you been hiding your light—don't tell me, pounding away at Rick's book, the slavedriver...'

The comments and compliments came thick and fast, and it was only when the band finally packed up and exhausted but happy couples began to drift away to bed that she came back to earth with a crash.

Rick was still there, at the bar, but as Evonne watched he put his arm around the pretty girl he was talking to and kissed her on the forehead, and they laughed together and went on talking.

Evonne closed her eyes and swayed where she stood as thought after frightening thought pounded at her brain, and she was conscious of never feeling more alone in her life. Alone and . . . jealous. Alone yet frighteningly alive, in a way she'd sworn would never happen to her again. Alive to the desire, the need to be loved.

She whirled on her heel and ran out of the lounge and down the path, uncaring of emus and kangaroos, ran all the way and up the stairs to her room, where she shut herself in and leant back against the door, breathing distractedly and saying over and over to herself, 'No, oh, no . . .'

CHAPTER FOUR

IT WAS a knock on the door that jerked her away from it as if burnt, and Rick saying her name, unmistakably Rick, although the sound was muffled.

'No,' she whispered yet again, and tiptoed into the main body of the room. She had left one bedside lamp on and she crossed over to it swiftly and switched it off. Then she sat down on the bed in the darkness wringing her hands, staring towards the door and praying he would go away.

He did after a time—at least, he stopped knocking, and she heard his own door close in the quiet of the night, and felt her chest muscles relax slightly.

Her relief was short-lived, however, because there was an unnaturally loud clatter on her moonlit veranda and she swung around, wide-eyed, to see Rick picking himself up from a welter of overturned chair and table.

Evonne sprang up, but he limped in through the glass doors before she could reach them, caught her wrists in one hand, while he slid the door closed with the other, swung the curtain closed too, then dragged her with him to switch on the bedside light.

'How dare you?' she panted, struggling desperately to free herself, not believing he was so strong. 'How *dare* you *climb* into my room like this?'

'I didn't do it from choice, believe me,' he said ironically. 'It was the only way to get to you—to break into your ivory tower,' he added almost contemptuously, and released her abruptly.

Evonne lost her balance and sat down awkwardly on the bed.

'Sorry,' he said immediately, 'but you might as well stay there.' He loomed over her so that she couldn't get up.

She glared at him and rubbed her wrists resentfully, prey to so many conflicting emotions that although she tried to speak, nothing came out.

He observed this for a moment, then said, 'What happened back there?' He gestured towards the main complex.

'Nothing!'

'Don't lie, Evonne,' he said curtly. 'One minute you were having the time of your life, the next you were literally running for cover. Did you suddenly realise how much you've broken your vows lately? Did it hit you that you were living and laughing—and loving it?'

Her eyes widened and her lips parted and her breath caught in her throat. 'H-how...' she stammered, then a look of horror clouded her eyes, and she twisted away and laid her head on the pillows. 'Go away,' she said hoarsely.

'No.'

She sat up convulsively. 'Then I will! I don't have to be ... interrogated by you, of all people.'

'Of all people? What's that supposed to mean?' queried Rick.

'It means,' she didn't realise her teeth were chattering, she didn't, somehow couldn't stop the words from tumbling out, 'don't let me keep you from the girl you were with, and planning to spend the night with, no d-doubt!'

'Jealous, Evonne?' he shot at her.

'*No* . . . oh!' she cried. 'Stop standing over me as if . . . as if . . .'

Rick moved away, but for some reason her legs felt as if they wouldn't be capable of supporting her, so she stayed where she was, breathing unsteadily, staring at the wall until she put her hands to her face and encountered her brave pink hibiscus blooms which were coming adrift and closing up anyway. She plucked them out impatiently and stared at them instead, then started to shred them, petal by petal.

'Evonne?'

'I wish you'd just go away,' she whispered.

He didn't answer, and for a few minutes, in her misery, she didn't care whether he went or stayed, whether she was dead or alive.

Then some sounds pierced her consciousness and she turned to see that he had boiled the electric jug each room was equipped with, and was making coffee. Her shoulders sagged and she sighed soundlessly, then watched helplessly as he put two gently steaming cups on the low table and arranged the two armchairs around it.

He straightened and stared at her for a moment, then said quietly, 'Come on.'

Evonne looked away, then stood up with a shrug.

The coffee was too hot, and she burnt her lips with the first sip and put the cup down jerkily so that it rattled against the saucer.

Rick said, into the silence that followed and with a wry glance around, 'Your room puts mine to shame.'

She looked around at the neatness. There were no clothes in sight, the dressing-table bore her cosmetics in beautiful, expensive jars and tubes and arranged like a display. There were no shoes on the floor, no towels lying about, not even a purse or a bag, and on her work-table no sign of his brown paper shopping bags but neat piles of foolscap, her typing paper, two pens; her type-writer was covered. The only evidence of any slight disorder was the scattering of torn pink petals on the bedspread—and a few still clinging to the front of her dress.

She picked one fragment up between her fingers and said huskily, 'Look, I'm sorry, I...got a bit carried away, but it's really nothing for you to worry about. It's not any of your...' She stopped and bit her lip.

'Business?' he supplied.

'Well,' she said with an effort, 'I don't mean to sound ungracious, but no, it isn't.'

Rick lay back in his chair and studied her thoughtfully from beneath half-closed lids, and while she held her breath, waiting for his reply, she noticed with a curious little ache around her heart that he had scratched the side of his face when he had tripped over her veranda furniture.

'I'm afraid I have to disagree,' he said at last.

'If you're worried about your book, I'll still finish it for you . . .'

'Evonne,' he said softly but compellingly and with an odd hint of menace, 'let's not beat about the bush any more. The way you are, the state you're in, affects me, and you know very well why.'

'Do I? I'm sorry to say I don't . . .'

'Yes, you do,' he countered. 'Oh, we've kept it under wraps—in fact you've done your best to bury it as deep as you can, and *because* of the curious way it appears to affect *you*, I've,' he shrugged, 'gone along with it. But none of that alters the fact that there's a rather primitive attraction between us, my dear.'

She made a protesting little sound, but he ignored it and went on, 'I'd even go so far as to say one of those spontaneous ones—it was certainly like that for me.'

Evonne stood up clumsily. 'I don't want to hear any more. I'm *not* interested . . .'

'Then why *are* you so bloody upset?' he interrupted coldly. 'And so uptight?'

'I'm . . .'

But he swore beneath his breath and got up in one long, lithe movement and before she could take evasive action, had her in his arms. 'Surely you couldn't be so beautiful,' he said, his lips barely moving and his green eyes seemingly raking her soul, 'and have no honesty in your heart. We want each other, Evonne. Whatever else is wrong for you, whatever is impossible about it, doesn't change that one simple fact.

Nothing can change the fact that you saw me with a girl and thought I was going to sleep with her tonight, and it hurt.'

'All right, it *hurt*,' she said through her teeth. 'But it wasn't only you—don't flatter yourself it was particularly *you*. It was...I was just suddenly desperately lonely. Everyone was going, everyone had a...partner, it...got to me, that's all.'

'Poor little Cinderella Evonne,' he mocked. 'What really interests me is why you're such a determined Cinderella, not to mention deliberately blind and...'

'Let me go, Rick,' she warned, and tried to break free.

'Not just yet, sweetheart,' he drawled. 'It seems I have a score to settle—my pride,' he added with a dry little smile, 'appears to be ruffled. Let's see how you kiss just anyone, not particularly *me*— if you follow my drift.'

Evonne gasped, but he only laughed quietly and drew her closer.

'I'll scream,' she threatened.

'Scream away,' he murmured, 'because I intend to kiss you, and while I concede that with words—well, you handle them with as much dexterity as a nasty sharp little dagger does its work— but in this I might just have the edge.'

She didn't scream, but she fought him with all her strength—and Rick resisted with as little of his as was necessary to keep her in his arms and pressed to the lean, hard length of him. She wrenched her mouth free and one arm and tried to hit him, but he caught her wrist and imprisoned her arm behind her back. He slid the fingers of his other hand through her hair and tugged her head back and claimed her mouth again, but once again she got it free. Then she started to swear at him, unprintable words she hated and always tried to forget she ever knew, words she had heard her drunken father say to her mother over and over again until he walked out on them all...

It was the quizzical spark of amusement in Rick's eyes that stopped the flow but, what was worse, her contempt for herself seemed to drain all the fight out of her, and that was when she fell into a terrible trap...

'Quite finished?' he said softly, and started to kiss her again.

Later, for ever afterwards, Evonne was to wonder if it was being drained not only spiritually by the unforgivable lapse in the smooth veneer of her sophistication, but also being physically close to exhaustion, that accounted for it. Accounted for the way she gradually found herself clinging to him rather than being held and restrained; found her heart beating erratically as he increased the pressure on her mouth and her lips parted and she was suddenly drowning in the taste of him, aware through every pore of the feel of his body against hers, conscious of her body as if the blood was singing through her veins and as if her breasts, her thighs, her throat craved for more than even this contact, needed his hands upon them, exploring, releasing the incredible tension beneath the surface of her skin, cupping, caressing...

She moaned beneath his mouth, a husky, unmistakable little sound of desire, and when he lifted his head, she could only lean her brow on his shoulder, shaken to the core, bereft.

She heard him say something dimly, but once heard, it was as if his quietly mocking words were engraved on her heart. 'So you like it rough, Patterson. I don't know if I should be surprised, but somehow I'm not.'

She moved convulsively and his arms fell away, but as their eyes met she trembled, knowing there was more to come.

There was. Rick took her hand and turned her so that they were facing the wide mirror above the dressing table. Evonne could only close her eyes after a moment at what she saw. Her hair was tumbling down, her cheeks were flushed, her strapless dress had slipped down a little at one side and her mouth was ripe. To complete her dishevelment, she was standing awkwardly at an angle because she had lost one shoe in her futile fight.

'Get out,' she whispered raggedly, kicking off the other one.

'Just going,' he said, and added meditatively, 'Yes, I think I always knew you were a case of still waters running deep. Goodnight, my dear.' And he left the way he had come, climbing over her veranda on to his because, he informed her casually, he had neglected to bring his key. He didn't trip over anything this time.

Evonne lay huddled on her bed, on top of the cover, still in her chalk-blue dress, for about an hour, staring with terrible eyes at the wall, hugging herself. Then she got up and had a shower, locked herself in and, secure in the knowledge that she had often typed very early and quite late without disturbing Rick or anyone else, set to work.

When the sun rose, she fortified herself with a cup of coffee and the thought that she had eaten enough last night to last her for a good few hours. By nine o'clock, seven hours of virtually straight, swift typing without any breaks to chuckle at or enjoy the manuscript, she was dizzy and seeing double, stiff and cramped, but it was finished. Wearily she clipped the last chapter together and slid the pile into an envelope folder. Then she got up, stretched and, with every step an effort, began to pack. Finally she took another shower and stood in it for an age, contemplating her options. There were several flights a day off the island, but if they were booked she could take the afternoon boat. All that remained was how to spend the intervening hours—and how to blank her mind to that dreadful question she kept asking herself. Had she been right . . . or was Rick right? Not that it mattered, she kept telling herself, not that it mattered.

She stepped out of the shower at last and dressed as if she was leaving there and then, in an almond safari dress with a woven straw belt and matching shoes, and she tied her hair back with a silk jade green scarf. The finished effect was perfectly groomed, but nothing could hide the shadows under her eyes, and her bag and sunglasses lay ready on the bed. Still, it was curiously hard to leave the security of her room to make the necessary arrangements—one disadvantage of Brampton was no phones in the rooms—and she was hesitating briefly when Rick knocked on the door.

She flinched and wondered foolishly if she would ever come to know anyone else's knock so well, then she squared her shoulders and went to answer it.

Nothing, she knew, could stop her blushing at the mere sight of him, leaning on her doorframe with his hand raised to knock again, looking tall and still sleepy about the eyes but as formally dressed as she had ever seen him. Formal for Rick, that was, she suspected, in a round-necked slate blue T-shirt beneath a check blue and grey seersucker sports jacket and grey pants.

They said nothing for a moment, as he watched the hot colour rise to her cheeks and Evonne steeled herself to say what she had to.

'Come in.'

He straightened and followed her in, and his eyes went immediately to her luggage standing neatly in the middle of the floor. 'I suspected as much,' he murmured.

'It was probably the suspectable thing,' Evonne returned drily.

'No, I mean I felt in my bones. Look at this.' He turned towards the door and gestured for her to go outside to the landing.

'What...?'

'Just have a look.'

She compressed her lips, then with a shrug went out to have a look. Rick followed her and indicated a pile of luggage outside his door.

Evonne blinked. 'You're... leaving too?' she said uncertainly.

'Uh-huh.'

'Why?'

'Can't you guess?'

'*No* ... I mean,' she turned and went back into her room, and he followed her, 'you don't have to. I've finished your book. It's all typed up.' She pointed to the bed. 'There's no need for you to leave yet.'

He stared at the pile on the bed and then at her with an incredulous frown growing in his eyes. 'You ... But when?'

'Last night,' she said briefly, then added more accurately, 'This morning.'

'Did you go to bed at *all*?'

She shrugged. 'No. So you see...'

'I don't see anything—*why*?' he interrupted roughly.

Evonne took a breath. 'I also,' she said steadily, 'like to complete any projects I undertake. And if you want me to be really honest,' she closed her eyes briefly at the sudden flash of anger in her voice but went on truthfully, 'I thought it might obviate the need for you to resort to any kind of blackmail...'

'Blackmail,' Rick said softly.

'Yes, *blackmail*...' She stopped and bit her lip. 'Authors are notorious for it,' she added coolly.

'Oh, that kind of blackmail,' he drawled. 'It so happens you're right.'

'Well, now there's no need...'

'Evonne,' he cut in, 'sit down, will you? There's something I have to tell you.'

'There's nothing I want to hear!'

'Don't make me have to force you, my dear,' he said quietly but with that sudden tiger-like glint in his green eyes.

Evonne hesitated, remembered and coloured faintly, then sat with as much dignity as she could muster. But I won't be manipulated into *anything*! she told herself grimly.

Rick stared at her for a moment, then sat down on the end of the bed and rubbed the side of his face gingerly, and she noticed for the first time that there was a faint bruise around one eye as well as the slight scratch.

Her lips parted. 'You've got a black eye,' she said involuntarily, then cursed herself.

'I know, from your veranda furniture.'

'It's not *mine*...' She broke off and gritted her teeth against any more inane comments. 'Go on,' she ordered, 'I haven't got all day.'

Rick smiled faintly and she found herself feeling hot again, hot and foolish, which always made her defensive and impossible—oh, why doesn't he just let me go? she wondered miserably.

'It's about my pride—and me,' he said slowly. 'We're in even more... disharmony than we were last night, so I have to tell you that I'm sorry for what happened.' His green eyes searched her face.

'Thanks,' she said stiffly. 'I appreciate...'

'On the other hand, I'm not going to let the matter go. And that's why, when I woke up this morning with this certainty in my mind that you were packing and determined to leave, I decided to come with you.'

'Come...?' Evonne stared at him, wide-eyed. 'I don't think I know what you mean. Where?'

'Wherever you go,' he said simply, with the absolute simplicity of utter conviction, in fact.

She sprang up. 'You're mad!' she said agitatedly. 'Quite mad. Why me, and after...why me?'

'I'm not quite sure,' Rick said meditatively. 'I mean, I've surprised myself somewhat. I generally fall for uninhibited, athletic blondes, but there's something so very different about you. You have a pale pearl glow, but it's mysteriously veiled as if through a mantilla—your personality as well as your beautiful body...'

'Stop it!' Evonne commanded hoarsely. 'Anyway, you *can't*...'

'Oh, but I can,' he returned mildly. 'I'm also a seeker of the truth—comes from being a geographer, no doubt—so I'm really interested to find out who is right in this matter, you or me.'

Evonne had been pacing the room incredulously, but she stopped as if shot.

'Ah,' he murmured, watching her, 'so you *have* wondered about that.'

'You're diabolical!' she breathed, then *could* have shot herself.

Rick shrugged. 'That's the other thing I'd like to get to the bottom of, why you are the way you are. What's so diabolical about it?'

'You...'

'But there'll be no coercion, I promise,' he overrode her. 'Last night was a slight aberration, as I've mentioned and apologised for. Where are you off to, incidentally? Back to Uncle Amos's bosom? That's no problem for me. I'll tell him you've achieved the impossible—in fact you accomplished your mission.'

'You w-wouldn't!' she stammered.

'I'd have no qualms about telling him that perhaps I ought to have a look at the business instead of rejecting it out of hand—who knows? It might even be the *wise* thing to do.'

'Your book,' whispered Evonne with the hollow, sinking certainty that she was trapped, that Rick would do exactly as he said. But it's...unbelievable! she told herself, then glanced at him and knew it was not. Not for a man who had just spent a year of his life buried beyond the last frontier amongst often hostile, unintelligible people in the cause of a science he believed in passionately.

'My book,' he repeated thoughtfully. 'Therein lies an alternative for us, Evonne.'

She sat down again and stared at him bleakly. 'Tell me,' she invited finally with a feeling of fatal fascination.

'It's too long.'

She raised an eyebrow. 'How do you know that?'

'I've spent enough years doing and correcting assignments to know that it's almost exactly seventy-five thousand words long, whereas sixty thousand is the length my publisher has in mind.'

'Do you mean to tell me I've typed fifteen thousand unnecessary words?'

He grinned. 'The problem was how to distinguish the unnecessary ones, and until it *was* typed...' He looked at her ruefully.

She was silent for a time, staring at her hands. Then she said with an effort, 'I don't see—it is typed now, and your editor will be the best person to...'

'No,' he said quietly and quite definitely. 'I'd rather you did it. You have the experience, you've laboured over it, from the odd things you've said I think it appeals to you... let *us* do it.'

'Rick...' Evonne stood up again and walked over to the windows. He stared at the slender line of her back, the chic, cool almond dress, and got up to stand behind her.

'Let's go to Sydney, Evonne,' he said very quietly. 'Sydney always makes me feel alive, I love it and I haven't seen it for twelve months. Let's feast ourselves on beautiful Sydney and see what comes of it.'

'Do I have a choice?' she whispered.

'No. But you have the choice of at least admitting that, for whatever reason, you kissed me last night like someone... starved, drowning...' she flinched and he lifted a hand to touch the brave green scarf on her hair ' ... someone tormented,' he went on. 'You can at least admit that, rather than go on being an emotional coward.'

She didn't stir, and his hand left her hair to lie lightly on her shoulder, then he turned her to face him.

She didn't resist, nor did she try to hide the fact that her eyes were bright with hot, stinging tears. 'So you think you can be my psychiatrist as well as my lover?' she said, licking the tears off her lip as they overflowed. 'Don't blame me when I remind you that it was *your* idea.'

Evonne slept quite a lot on the way to Sydney, unusual for her in aircraft, but because it was broken not only by meals but landing in Rockhampton and Brisbane, she arrived feeling like a zombie. Then Rick's 'beautiful Sydney' was cloaked with thick, dark cloud and it was pouring on the ground. They had hardly talked at all since leaving Brampton.

'I've booked us into the Inter-Continental,' Rick told her in the taxi. 'Separate rooms but next door. Do you know it?'

'Yes. It's rather lovely—they've preserved the old Treasury building for the first couple of floors. It's also expensive.'

'Don't worry about it,' he told her.

'Why separate rooms?'

He glanced at her, then said deliberately, 'My idea was not for us to sleep together in the spirit of your saying—you wanted it, you've got it...for what it's worth.'

She looked out of the window at the teeming rain and suppressed a shiver. 'It's not worth a lot.'

Rick didn't answer, and when she turned back to him there was a glint of anger in his green eyes. But he only said, 'Perhaps you should let others be the judge of that.'

Evonne shrugged.

The Inter-Continental was fairly new, but Evonne had stayed there a couple of times on business trips to Sydney, and been genuinely captivated. She loved the Cortile, the foyer lounge, raised up a few steps in the middle of the restored old Treasury, surrounded by arched galleries of old pink stone and beneath a skylight dome. She loved the old lift cages, no longer in use but preserved, and the atmosphere that was reminiscent of grand hotels of bygone eras in far-flung parts of the world, crossroads where you might see the rich and famous, even infamous. She had noted on her previous stays that there always seemed to be a cross-section of the world Press staying at the Inter-Continental, drinking coffee in the Cortile and scribbling in their notebooks.

None of this, as they booked in, gave her the usual lift of spirits, and she realised she had passed from the physical discomfort of exhaustion to a state of numbness. Their rooms were on the twenty-first floor, with views over Farm Cove, the Botanical Gardens and the Harbour towards the Heads—or they would be, she knew, when the rain cleared. But the rain was heavy and steady, as heavy as her heart.

She stared at her bags and the thought of unpacking was equally heavy.

'Don't,' said Rick behind her, and he walked round her to inspect her face. 'Will you be able to sleep, do you think?'

Evonne shook her head dumbly, then made an effort. 'I shouldn't have danced so energetically on top of...on top of everything else. I feel as if I'm dancing again. That's crazy, but...'

'Then I've got a better idea.' He disappeared into the bathroom and she heard the taps being run. Then he opened her fridge and inspected the mini-bar, poured two brandies and soda, more brandy than soda, and handed her one. 'Take it into the bath with you, sip it while you soak, relax your muscles one by one—I've poured some bubble bath in, take your time.'

'I'm going!'

The bath was heavenly, and she soaked for half an hour, sipping as ordered, until her eyelids began to feel heavy and she forced herself out reluctantly. She dried herself lethargically, then stopped to stare at herself in the mirror. Her loose, thick hair, usually so sleek, had curled in little tendrils about her face from the steam and her body was pink and glowing—her body that had betrayed her so completely last night that she could still feel it, still remember.

She closed her eyes and reached for the thick white towelling gown behind the door.

Rick had not gone as she had half expected but was lying back on the settee with his feet up on a glass-topped table and the afternoon paper in his hands. But her bags had disappeared and the bed was turned down invitingly.

He looked up and cocked an eyebrow at her. 'Feeling better?'

'Yes. What...?' Evonne looked around, mystified.

'I unpacked for you,' he said casually. 'I remembered what you said about respecting your clothes, and anyway, this is my kind of hotel.'

'It is? I don't see what that's got to do with it.'

'They have proper hangers.'

Evonne stared at him, then swung round to open the built-in wardrobe. And there were all her clothes hanging up neatly on proper hangers.

'Underwear here,' said Rick, opening a drawer beneath the television, 'miscellaneous on this side.' Miscellaneous included belts and scarves. 'I didn't unpack your make-up because I thought the best place for it might be the bathroom...what's so funny?'

'I don't know,' she gasped, and sat down on the side of the bed, then lay back against the pillows. 'Sometimes you really surprise me, that's all. Oh, I'm so tired!'

'Will you sleep now?' He pulled the bed-clothes up and bent over her.

'Yes, yes,' she said drowsily. 'I nearly fell asleep in the bath.'

'Do you want to change into a nightgown? You have more beautiful nightgowns than I've ever seen before.'

'No, I'm fine, I haven't got the energy...' And indeed, she found she couldn't keep her eyes open. Not even when she felt his lips brush her brow.

'Sleep easy, Cinderella.'

'Goodnight.'

Nor did she know that he watched and waited until her breathing was quiet and regular and her hand, which had been curled up on the pillow, slowly relaxed and opened. If she had, she would have seen the frown in Rick's eyes as he studied her unconscious, naked face for quite a few minutes before he quietly left.

She woke up once, very late, and lay still, getting her bearings, then finding her thoughts turning to Rick like a quiet stream that would not be diverted. A man she barely knew, she thought, then had to qualify it. Through his book, if for no other reason, I do know him, but not half as well as he seems to know me. What...what am I letting myself in for? If I can't back out at this stage, somehow, what will...what is the only way it will ever end? The way it always does. I must think...

But sleep claimed her again, insidiously, a silent enemy with weapons she had no answer for. Rather like Rick himself, was her last thought.

CHAPTER FIVE

HER phone rang at eight-thirty, waking her.

It was Rick with the news that he had ordered breakfast for them both, it was outside her door, and could he come and eat with her?

Evonne said yes, and almost immediately a knock sounded on the door. So it was that, still clad in the towelling robe and with dishevelled hair and barely awake, she went to open the door, to be greeted by not one but two specimens of keen-eyed, shaved and alert masculinity, one of them Rick and one of them the room-service waiter, who was not only keen-eyed but extremely genial.

'It's a lovely day, madam,' he said as he pushed his trolley in. 'May I open the curtains for you? Sydney is just blooming this morning—you won't be sorry to see it!'

'Please do,' Evonne smiled and he was right. There was no sign of the cloud and rain of the previous day, the waters of the Harbour were pale blue and everything else, suburbs, gardens, the hydrofoil streaking towards Manly and leaving a delicate white curved wake upon the pale blue, stood out with the extra clarity of a new, fine day.

Evonne sat on the side of the bed as the trolley was expertly converted to a table, napkins were flourished and orange juice poured, feeling slightly overcome and not altogether in tune with her surroundings or her company.

'Drink this,' advised Rick, handing her a glass of orange juice as the waiter finally left. 'I know how you feel.'

'Do you?' She took the glass and their fingers brushed briefly.

'For a little while after sleeping for over twelve hours, it's almost as bad as before you went to bed. I ordered you an omelette, by the way—you must be starving.'

Evonne studied him over the top of her glass. The bruise around his eye was slightly darker, but the scratch had healed. He wore grey jeans and a green cotton-knit shirt with a white collar, open at the throat, his hair was damp and un- usually tidy—and once again she was struck by the fact that he seemed younger than she was. Younger and carefree and the least likely-looking prospective Doctor of Geography she could im- agine. That's the problem with him, she mused, and drank some orange. You *think* he's just another elegant young man who attracts girls like bees to a honeypot, and thoroughly enjoys it, then you run into the...other side of him. Why do I feel...so helpless?

'Come,' Rick said as he had before. 'Your omelette awaits you, madam.'

Her omelette was stuffed with tiny little mush- rooms and was delicious. Then he poured her coffee, and the aroma was strong, and she tilted her head back and breathed deeply and appreciatively.

'Reckon you might live now?' he asked with a grin.

'Yes, but I feel such a mess.' Evonne raised her arms and ran her hands through her hair.

'I'm sure no one can rectify that as exquisitely as you, although your idea of a mess isn't mine.'

'Rick.' She sat forward and sipped her coffee. 'I...'

'Why don't we give ourselves a break today?' he interrupted.

Evonne put the cup down and fiddled with the handle, staring at it, then lifted her dark eyes to his. 'A break from what?'

Rick thought before he spoke, then said with an oddly intent glance, 'Trauma, drama—that kind of thing. Too much thought or reasoning. Why don't we just let our senses take over?'

Her fingers curled rather tightly round the delicate handle of her coffee-cup. 'If you mean...'

'I mean—when you're ready and you can take all the time in the world—why don't we wander down to Circular Quay and take the Taronga Park ferry to the Zoo? It'll be beautiful on the Harbour, and zoos fascinate me. We could wander around slowly, have some lunch there, commune with nature, talk...about everything but us, if you prefer.'

Evonne uncurled her fingers. 'The Zoo,' she said softly.

A gleam lit his green eyes. 'You like the Zoo, too?'

'I...every year on Boxing Day we used to go to the Zoo. It was the highlight of Christmas, sometimes the whole year. We used to work ourselves into a fever pitch of excitement, and afterwards, we'd be so thoroughly overtired we'd fight and Mum would say, "Right! That's the last time I ever take you lot to the Zoo!" But every year she came up trumps, somehow.'

She stared across the room but seeing into the past, seeing the last time she'd been to the Zoo, at fifteen and as the oldest, carrying Sandra, the baby of the family at six, awkwardly on her hip and with Sam, eight, on the other side, held by the hand in a vicelike grip because of his tendency to wander off and get lost—and a smile curved her lips.

'Tell me,' Rick said quietly.

She shrugged slightly. 'We were such riff-raff. Poor Mum!'

'How many of you?'

'Six—I was just thinking of the last time, the last Boxing Day when I was fifteen—I never went again.'

'Why not?'

'That was the year I lost my innocence,' she said meditatively. 'Oh,' as his eyes widened, 'not like that, that took another few years, but during that year I suddenly stopped . . . being a child, I guess. I began to become embarrassed by the riff-raff we were, which was odd, because up until then if anyone said a word against us, I'd fight them tooth and nail. But then, that year, that was when the longing to get away, the determination not to be sucked into the poverty and the . . . everything else that seemed to be self-perpetuating, started to crystallise. I don't suppose you know what it's like to be poor?' she finished.

Rick didn't answer immediately, and the curious notion took hold of Evonne that she could see the wheels of his mind absorbing this fact about her and placing it in context. I bet he's saying to himself—ah, that's one reason she's the way she is. Then again, I am...

'No,' he said at last. 'And you've succeeded, you've fulfilled those fifteen-year-old dreams, obviously.'

'Oh yes. Yes!'

'If it's going to be painful to go to the Zoo we could...'

'I think I'd like nothing better than to go to the Zoo today,' said Evonne, and smiled at him. 'You have some very good ideas sometimes. But tomorrow...' She stopped as something settled in her mind like a leaf falling, a silent sigh, and she knew she had given in to this battle she should be waging without a fight, put off until tomorrow what she should have done today. Why the Zoo? she wondered helplessly. How does he do it? How does he know I could have resisted just about anything but the Zoo—why can't I resist Taronga Park Zoo? Do I think I'll find that innocence again by going back?

'Tomorrow?' queried Rick with a lift of an eyebrow.

'I think I'd better wait before I pass judgement on tomorrow,' she told him.

'Very wise,' he commented. 'Just my philosophy, in fact.'

She blinked and thought of something cutting to say, but restrained herself. 'I'll get ready, then,' she said instead, and stood up.

'I'll leave you to it.'

She wore a pair of candy pink and white striped slacks, pink canvas espadrilles and a loose white blouse. She left her hair loose, brushed back and tucked behind her ears, and in her light canvas shoulder-bag carried only the barest of necessities—a brush, hanky, sunglasses, some money and a floppy linen hat. She couldn't help but be aware that she looked not only younger but touristy, possibly even eager, nor for the life of her could she care.

It appeared that Rick approved of this image, because in the lift he studied her until she started to colour faintly, then drawled, 'I like it.' All he carried was a camera.

'It's changed!' exclaimed Evonne.

'That's the sixth time you've said that.'

'But *cable cars*, and . . . it's smaller.'

'Perhaps you're just a big girl now, because it's not smaller.'

'I know,' she said ruefully. 'Oh, look, what's over there?'

Two hours later Rick insisted they stop for lunch, saying wryly, 'No wonder you all tired yourselves out—we haven't missed a single cage or enclosure or animal or species, and we're only half-way down yet! *I'm* exhausted.'

'I'll buy you lunch, then—no, please let me! We used to long to be able to *buy* lunch, but we always brought a picnic to save money—aren't kids hard to please?'

'Well, there's a bistro over there, but...'

'No, no, you don't come to the Zoo to go to a bistro,' Evonne told him scornfully. 'It's chips and tomato sauce, rubbery chicken pieces...well, perhaps you're right,' she conceded with a laugh. 'All the same, it's on me.'

It was at the elephant enclosure with its gaily painted pagoda that Rick said as they leant on the railing and Evonne watched the elephants fascinatedly, 'You're enjoying this trip down memory lane—it's good to see.'

She turned away and raised her face to the sun, closing her eyes. 'I've been like a kid let loose in a candy store. I really don't know why the fascination hasn't changed. You'd have thought it would...bring back the memories you've tried to forget for so long.'

'Perhaps they just don't have the power to hurt you any more.'

'Perhaps...' And she wondered about that.

Not long afterwards they came to the giraffes, one of which was a baby, and not only that...

'Look!' Evonne exclaimed delightedly. 'His name's Ricky. Now we both have namesakes!' And she insisted Rick take photos of the baby giraffe from all angles.

But finally they reached the bottom and caught the ferry again, and finally, as she stared across the water towards Mrs Macquarie's Chair and Wolloomooloo Bay with its fringe of grey-painted navy vessels, after she had pointed and told him

NO RISK, NO OBLIGATION TO BUY...NOW OR EVER!

GUARANTEED

PLAY "ROLL A DOUBLE" AND GET AS MANY AS FIVE GIFTS!

HERE'S HOW TO PLAY:

1. Peel off label from front cover. Place it in space provided at right. With a coin, carefully scratch off the silver dice. This makes you eligible to receive one or more free books, and possibly a gift, depending on what is revealed beneath the scratch-off area.

2. You'll receive brand-new Harlequin Presents® novels. When you return this card, we'll rush you the books and gift you qualify for ABSOLUTELY FREE!

3. Then, if we don't hear from you, every month we'll send you 6 additional novels to read and enjoy. You can return them and owe nothing, but if you decide to keep them, you'll pay only $2.24* per book - a savings of 26¢ each off the cover price. And, there's no extra charge for postage and handling!

4. When you subscribe to the Harlequin Reader Service®, you'll also get our newsletter, as well as additional free gifts from time to time.

5. You must be completely satisfied. You may cancel at any time simply by sending us a note or a shipping statement marked "cancel" or by returning any shipment to us at our expense.

*Terms and prices subject to change without notice. Sales tax applicable in N.Y. and Iowa.
©1990 Harlequin Enterprises Limited.

that was where she had grown up, the past did come back to haunt her and she went quiet.

They walked back to the hotel, and Rick suggested tea or whatever she wanted in the Cortile.

'All right, but I feel a bit of a wreck.'

He took her hand in a surprisingly hard grip. 'You look fine, you'd look fine in a sack—you don't have to scuttle away and change into some beautiful outfit and wear it like a suit of armour.'

Evonne bit her lip and followed him reluctantly.

Tea, though, she decided gratefully, was worth its weight in gold as a restorative, and it even enabled her to answer fairly serenely when he said, 'If you're reliving those memories now, let's share them. Why were you poor?'

'Because of broken dreams, probably. My parents both came from the country, they'd married young and come to Sydney to make their fortune, but they were no match for the city— not my father anyway, apparently—and he became a drunk and a wife-beater—perhaps he always would have been, I don't know. My mother was, still is, one of those naïve, timid women who accepted it all, had six children in quick succession despite the bashings—or perhaps because of them—and when the youngest was two, he walked out. Just left and was never heard of again. Funnily enough, that's when she became a tower of strength. Lord knows how she coped, but she did. We all stayed together, we never starved, we all went to school regularly. . .

And despite that incredible feat, she still is a gentle soul and constantly surprised by the hard, cruel facts of life.'

'But you were not?'

Evonne smiled. 'No. I became angry and...brash and intense, and it probably broke her heart to see me like that. But I just knew I wasn't going to get trapped, as she'd been, although, when I was about seventeen and a half, my hormones or whatever deluded me temporarily into thinking along those lines.'

'I know the feeling,' said Rick.

'Do you?'

He half smiled. 'For what it's worth, my parents were not well suited, although they stayed together and fought it out—discreetly, nevertheless it was all rather deadly. I think *I* was about eighteen when I fell seriously in love for the first time, very seriously, which amazed me a little because I thought I was very cynical about love and marriage. Perhaps you go through a superior stage where you assume *you* can do it right.'

Evonne blinked, then grimaced. 'I think you *might* be right. What happened?'

'She threw me over for a French tennis player, a real cad and not in the least serious,' he grinned. 'And you?'

'I don't know what he threw me over for, he simply left, but I can guess—I was also so serious about it all. Fortunately his doing it like that, just walking away, really rang the warning bells and I saw,' she shrugged, 'the real difficulty— how to break the mould that, just by being there, at home and even loving my mother fiercely and admiring her, was all the same setting me on the same path.'

'Have you ever allowed your "hormones" free rein again?'

Evonne looked across at him steadily and said quietly, 'That tea was just what I needed. You know, I think if I sat down for a couple of hours with your manuscript, I could come up with some suggestions.'

'I thought we'd agreed today was to be sacred?'

'Rick, don't push your luck!'

'Rick!' a strange voice said over them. 'Good lord, it is you! How was Papua? How long have you been back in town—and of course! Should I get down on one knee, Sir Richard?'

'Don't you dare,' Rick said laughingly, and got up to shake the tall bearded man by the hand, then he turned to Evonne. 'This is Basil Brush—no, not really, Basil Mackenzie, a colleague of mine, Evonne. Evonne Patterson, Baz.'

'How do you *do*, Miss Patterson? This is really most fortuitous, Rick. Several of us are gathered in town tonight for a dinner—why don't you and Evonne join us? We'd be delighted . . . how long have you been back in town, old son? And why have you neglected your alumni mates—but never mind, we can rectify that tonight. Are you staying here?'

'Yes, but I've afraid we can't, Baz. Evonne and I are already spoken for this evening, such a pity,' drawled Rick.

'Oh . . . um . . . I get you,' said Basil Mackenzie with a wink and a nudge. 'So long as your new-found eminence hasn't . . .'

'Where are you dining?' Rick broke in. 'We might look in later.'

'Zollies . . . yes, do that, old son. Delighted to have met you, Evonne! And don't let him forget, will you?'

Evonne found herself hiding a smile, for several reasons. One of them was Rick's expression as Basil retreated. 'Not one of your favourite people,' she commented when he was out of earshot.

Rick sat down and smiled reluctantly, 'A perpetual schoolboy type! At least we know where not to dine tonight, or even be within a half-mile radius. Do *you* have any preference in the matter?'

'I . . . no. Rick . . .'

'Evonne, humour me in this,' he said with a suddenly dangerous glint in his eyes. 'All I'm asking you is to have dinner with me, not go to bed with me.'

'The one is often the prelude to the other, though,' she retorted.

'I swear I won't be so obvious—or naïve,' he stated with a flash of very genuine irritation. 'Haven't you enjoyed yourself today?'

'Yes, of course. Thank you,' Evonne said a little disjointedly, then added more thoughtfully, 'If I've succeeded in thoroughly annoying you, though, I don't think it's such a good idea to have . . .'

'You're not the only reason I'm annoyed,' he interrupted.

'Oh?' She raised her eyebrows.

'Although your calm assumption that you've succeeded in annoying me without even trying—as if I were an irrational schoolboy,' he marvelled, 'is even more annoying!'

'We seem to be having an impossible conversation,' Evonne said quietly, and gathered her bag and sunglasses.

'From which you're about to run away, no doubt,' Rick said harshly.

She glanced at him and caught her breath inwardly, because although he looked angry, he also looked intensely alive, and some of that—even irate—vitality was mysteriously transferring itself to her, starting to leap in her veins. I'd love to have a thorough row with you, Rick Emerson, she found herself thinking, a thorough, cleansing row. I'd love to tell you you're being childish, I'd enjoy getting really mad with you—but no, you've made me play that game before, with disastrous results. No!

'All right, I will have dinner with you—if you tell me what else has upset you,' she said mildly.

Rick's expression defied description for an instant—other than fitting the distinctly murderous label. Then in a lightning change of mood he was laughing, and she couldn't help laughing a little with him and at him, at them, and it was warm and companionable...

'My friend and colleague, Basil Brush, is the other cause,' he said at last. 'He'll spread the word that I'm back—you see!'

'Does it matter so much?'

'Yes, damn it, it does. I had hoped to escape detection for a while longer.'

'You know so many people in Sydney?'

'I live here,' he said.

'Well,' Evonne paused, 'yes, I'd forgotten... Where?'

'Nowhere.'

'Then...?'

'At present. I gave up my house when I went to New Guinea. I'll have to find somewhere else to rent, if I decide to stay.'

'Sydney,' she observed, 'mightn't have been the place to come, then, if you didn't want to meet people you knew.'

'In the heat of the moment it seemed like a good idea, and I assured myself it was such a big city... however, be that as it may, have I really redeemed myself sufficiently for you to have dinner with me?'

'Yes,' she said promptly, 'but you choose— this is your city, after all. May I be allowed to change?'

Rick sat back and a smile twisted his lips. 'You know what I'd like?' he said with a meditative little gleam in his green eyes. 'I think I'd like to be treated to a full production Patterson tonight, so get out your glad rags and we'll do the town.'

'I thought you disapproved... of my motive behind getting dressed up?' said Evonne with a genuine touch of indignation.

'I might—but I also have a genuine appreciation for a work of art.'

Evonne stared at him and felt that sensation of a leaf falling like a silent sigh in her mind again, and she thought, he's impossible, he's downright dangerous, and the longer I stay with him, the harder it's going to be. Tonight, it has to be tonight.

'You asked for it,' she said almost gently. 'But I need time, these things can't be rushed.'

Rick glanced at his watch. 'Two hours? It's nearly six o'clock, believe it or not.'

'That will be ample.' She stood up. 'I'll expect you at eight. No, don't come up with me, you can't possibly need two hours yourself—anyway, there's someone else approaching with a distinctly——' she was looking over his head '— *"Good lord, it's Rick!"* expression.' She smiled as he closed his eyes, and made her escape.

Once in the safety of her room, Evonne closed the door and leant back on it for a moment, then she pushed herself away and wandered around, her mind moving in strange circles.

Then she set to work.

Rick came for her at eight o'clock precisely—and surprised her. He was wearing a cream jacket, black trousers, a white dinner shirt with a stand-up collar with turn-down points and a narrow black bow tie. His golden hair gleamed beneath the light and his eyes glinted very green—even more so, Evonne thought as they rested on her.

He said softly, 'Black becomes you—I always thought it suited blondes best, but now I know

I was wrong. It's your beautiful pale skin—how wise you were not to get a tan.'

'I'm not as pale as usual,' she said foolishly because her treacherous senses were reeling a little beneath the tall, oddly austere impact of him.

'Brampton added a glow, that's all,' he said, and reached for her hand. 'Ready?'

'Yes.'

In the mirror-panelled lift, Evonne stared at herself, at her beautiful silk satin dinner dress, so plain and elegant but made sensuous by the material, and the diamond brooch and earrings she wore, presents from Rick's uncle after the first successful year of the catalogue. Then she looked away from the picture they made together, her head just topping his shoulder, and looked down at the gleam of her skin beneath the dark, frosted stockings, at her shoes sprayed with diamanté, at her black satin bag held before her in both hands, and her gleaming garnet nails that exactly matched her lips and the velvet bow that secured her hair—and commanded herself to bear in mind at all times what she had to do tonight.

They ate superb little Sydney rock oysters, then steak that was charred on the outside, pink and melt-in-the-mouth on the inner, with a crisp, fresh side salad. They drank a Traminer Riesling that was light and fresh and laughingly declined dessert. Then they left the restaurant and walked a few blocks through the revitalising night air to a piano bar which was dim and the music soft, and Rick ordered coffee which was freshly ground and headily aromatic, and brandies.

'I'll be tipsy soon,' said Evonne, swirling her balloon glass.

'No, you won't.'

'How can you be so sure?'

'Because we're going to dance.'

She started to say something, but was forestalled by a band she hadn't seen arriving starting up and some double doors swinging back to reveal a gleaming parquet floor, lights flickering, and the music taking on a beat that would be, she knew, her downfall...

She said instead, 'You're too clever for me sometimes. First the Zoo and now this!'

Rick smiled slightly. 'The Zoo was a shot in the dark.'

She lowered her lashes and stared at the brandy, then swept him a look full of humour.

'Is that an invitation to do my damnedest?' he queried.

'Perhaps.'

He put his hand over hers on the table. 'Then I accept. Shall we dance?'

Evonne was very quiet when they finally left the bewitching music and walked back to the hotel hand in hand, still united by the music, by the feel of each other and the closeness they had shared, the way he had watched and tended her helpless surrender to the rhythm that was in her blood, she sometimes thought, but not only that, her surrender to him...

'Tired?' he asked once.

'Yes.'

They collected their keys, but Rick didn't leave her at her door, as she knew he wouldn't. He took her key from her suddenly nerveless fingers, opened her door and led her in by the hand.

There was a bright, white moon shedding its silver light over Sydney and pouring into her room, so he didn't switch on any lamps, and when she tensed and knew she had foolishly left her run to the last minute, that she was staring the failure of her resolution in the face, he drew two small objects from his pockets.

'I got these for us.'

'What...what are they?' Her voice was unsteady and husky.

'Our totems.' He put first one and then the other into her palm.

Evonne bent her head to study them, and found her heart beating slowly suddenly and with almost unbearable affection. They were two small carved wooden animals, an emu and a giraffe, and into their bases were printed their names, Evonne and Rick.

'Where...how?' she asked wonderingly.

'At the Zoo. Remember when you went to the Ladies'? I went into the gift shop. I...added their names myself.'

'I think it should be a "Y"...Yvonne, but...oh, Rick,' she whispered, as he put a hand on her hair and released the garnet velvet bow, 'you're so sweet—but,' she raised her face to his, 'I'm not the one for you. I've been trying to tell you all evening, and now...and now...' She stopped helplessly.

His fingers left her hair and caressed her cheek. 'What makes you so sure of that?' he asked very quietly.

'Because I know myself too well. I ... I'm older ...'

'I hesitate to contradict you, but my guess is that you're three—four years *younger*?'

'Three—in years, but in other ways I'm older at heart. I'm disillusioned and I'm hard-boiled, I'm cynical and ... let me go, *please*!'

'I can't,' Rick said even more quietly, and drew her into his arms. 'How much older did you feel tonight when you danced with me, when you really let yourself go and danced *for* me, *because* it was me, not only the music?'

Evonne caught her breath.

'You did, didn't you? It was different tonight, the way you danced, and you knew it. It was us, not just you and the music.'

She felt a flush of colour mount in her cheeks. 'I'm sorry, I shouldn't have ...' But she stopped with a little gasp as his arms tightened mercilessly about her and he said in a cold, hard voice, 'Sometimes you go too far, Evonne.'

'Oh, Rick,' she said shakily, 'if only I could make you understand!'

He released her abruptly and turned away from her, shoving his hands violently into his pockets. 'I think I do—at least, I think I understand what you're deluding yourself about.'

She licked her lips as he turned back to her suddenly. 'You're trying to say, aren't you, that— *I'm* not the one for you. *That's* it, isn't it, Evonne?' His lips curled sardonically and he shot out a hand and flicked on a lamp with savage impatience.

'Is there a difference?' she asked, blinking dazedly.

'Yes,' he said through his teeth. 'And to add insult to injury, you're no doubt blaming your hormones for the way you feel in my arms, the way your body reacts beneath my hands, your mouth beneath my lips. Don't look like that— there can only be one explanation, can't there? You might as well tell me who he is and why you can't have him.'

Evonne closed her eyes. 'I thought you said today was sacred.'

Rick swore. 'Sacred to us—not to the memory of some man you won't let yourself forget.'

'There is no *us*...'

'Oh, but there is,' he drawled, and moved towards her again.

She stiffened. 'Rick, you promised, you *said*...'

'I said I wouldn't be so obvious or naïve as to *assume* you would sleep with me tonight.'

'You also said, no drama or trauma—something about that.' She stared at him, her eyes dark and tormented, her face paler than usual, her lips trembling.

'You've obviously chosen to forget what else I said...although you danced with me with all your senses,' grated Rick, and his green eyes were brilliant and cruelly taunting.

She put her hands to her face, then realised she was still holding his totems. And sudden tears brimmed as she looked at them, brimmed and overflowed.

He said, 'Am I right, Evonne?'

She swallowed. 'No...'

'You don't lie very convincingly, my dear. He must have been a real bastard to leave you like this—the way you are.'

Before she even saw the trap, Evonne reacted instinctively and in the same manner she would have ten years ago, and by the time she stopped to draw breath it was too late—she'd not only given herself away in an unmistakable defence but she had cursed Rick Emerson again in the rough, tough language he and only he seemed to be able to draw from her after all these years.

She stopped with her breath catching in her throat, her lips working, her loose hair subsiding like a dark curtain, and the colour rose in her cheeks at the cool, absent smile twisting his lips, the quizzical light in his green eyes she remembered only too well.

And when he drawled, 'That's better—I like the way you...er...pull no punches when you get riled!' she only just restrained herself from screaming with frustration, and turned away precipitately, only to trip and have to bear the ignominy of having him catch her.

'Let me go!' she panted.

'In a minute—don't exhaust yourself, we've been there and done this once before, if you recall.'

'*You*...' But she couldn't break his grip on her shoulders, and finally she flung her head back and stared at him mutinously, contemptuously, her lips clamped tightly shut.

He laughed softly. 'I wouldn't dream of trying it,' he mocked, 'but one day I will because you'll want me to, you won't be able to help yourself, and none of the excuses you're concocting to explain the way I affect you will work any more—and none of the ashes of this dead love you carry in your heart will help you then, Evonne.'

'I wouldn't count on it if I were you!' she spat at him.

Rick smiled faintly. 'That's only because you don't really know what a persistent *bastard* I can be, as well as all the other kinds you tell me I am. You really have a most colourful vocabulary!' He released her suddenly and involuntarily she crossed her arms and her hands crept up towards her shoulders. To her amazement, she still had the emu and the giraffe in one hand, and in an angry, stony gesture, she held them out to him.

He ignored them and said abruptly, 'I'm sorry if I hurt you—or am I? Perhaps that's just the nature of things between us—extreme frustration. Incidentally, don't feel constrained to sit up all night editing my book, will you? And if you decide to pack up and run again, I won't be far behind.'

She stared at him and said just one despairing word, *'Why?'*

'I thought I told you how I feel about unfinished business,' he murmured, and he put his hand over her still outstretched one and closed it over the two little wooden animals. 'You keep them. Take *them* to bed with you.'

CHAPTER SIX

EVONNE awoke the next morning at nine-thirty.

She sat up, brushing the hair out of her eyes, and was conscious immediately of a feeling of unease and of being overburdened even before the events of the previous night fell into place in her mind. Then she lay back on her side with a sigh, gripping the corner of the pillow and staring at another bright new day through the open curtains she had neglected to close last night. It was a few minutes before she noticed the message light blinking on her phone.

She stared at it for a full minute before picking up the receiver.

'Yes, Miss Patterson,' the concierge said. 'The message reads—''Please meet me in the Cortile at eleven a.m. with the manuscript.'' It's signed ''Emerson''.'

'Thank you,' answered Evonne. She thought of ordering breakfast, winced as she remembered the way she'd started the day yesterday, and got up and made herself a cup of tea instead. Then she soaked in the bath, trying not to think but with the same thought circling her mind— was this the end? Had Rick, after last night and with the rest of the night to either sleep on it or think it over, decided to give up after all?

If so, why am I not rejoicing? she asked herself. Even if he's right about me, there's no future for us. What am I thinking? He's *not* right—he's just dangerously attractive, and I'm...it's been a long time, and perhaps it takes a very long time to put your senses to rest...

'Oh, *hell*!' she muttered, and climbed abruptly out of the bath.

She dressed very conservatively in a dull clay-pink, straight linen skirt and a long-sleeved white silk blouse. Her leather shoes matched the skirt but had wooden heels and she wore a string of tiny carved, polished wooden beads. She put her hair up simply and severely. But she still had nearly an hour to kill, she found, and with a sudden burst of resentment, she decided to pack. But even that left her with half an hour, and she sat down on the bed with Rick's manuscript in her lap and leafed through it until finally it was five to eleven. Still she hesitated, staring at the little wooden animals on the table beside the bed, and she reached out to touch them, but her hand fell back and she got up hastily, snatched up her shoulder-bag and the manuscript and left the room.

Rick was sitting with an older man, deep in conversation as Evonne approached, and only when she was right upon them did they look up.

For an instant her eyes clashed with Rick's, and in that instant, she knew that nothing had changed from last night, knew that his mood was impatient and dangerous and his eyes were very green and tiger-like.

She tensed inwardly as both men stood up and Rick drawled, 'This is Patterson, Len. She's my...' He stopped and subjected Evonne to a narrowed, satirical look. 'I don't quite know *how* to describe it, we have this rather tortured relationship, you see. The minder of my manuscript as well as my...other aspirations,' he finished, then added with a suddenly malicious glint in his eyes, 'Yes, my minder. This is Len Woodward, Evonne—my editor.'

Evonne could not control the faint flush of humiliation creeping up her throat, but she contrived to ignore it and accept Len Woodward's hand, even murmur, 'How do you do?' although she was smarting inwardly.

Len Woodward, however, was used to Rick's ways, apparently, because he held Evonne's hand in both of his and said with a warm smile, 'I gather he got out of bed on the wrong side this morning. I'm very happy to meet you, Evonne, and I believe I owe you a large debt of gratitude. I'm sure it was no small task rendering the masterpiece legible!'

'Do sit down, Evonne,' Rick invited. 'Tea? Coffee? Or something stronger?'

'Coffee, thank you,' she told him.

'Rick tells me you've had some experience in this game, and that he thinks you could edit it down to the length we have in mind...'

'She might have changed her mind about that,' Rick put in lazily, and subjected Evonne to a bland look of enquiry.

Evonne gripped her hands in her lap. 'I do have one or two ideas,' she said to Len Woodward. 'But I'm sure you don't need an amateur—and I really am—to tell you...'

'Did you make a copy?' Len Woodward broke in keenly.

'Yes, I did, but . . .'

'Then here's my suggestion. You keep one, I'll take one—you do your editing and I'll do mine, and we'll see what we come up with. I promise,' he turned to Rick, 'to listen to Evonne's suggestions if they differ from mine, and of course your preferences, but I should point out, the final say *is* mine.'

Rick opened his mouth to answer, but Evonne said quietly, 'You really can't argue with that.'

He shot her a green look that said, Can't I? then seemed to think better of it and said to Len Woodward with a wry grin, 'Is this what's called humouring the author?'

'Something like that,' the other man agreed. 'But I would also be interested to hear Evonne's ideas. You seem to be so sure they'll be good.'

Rick smiled twistedly and shrugged, 'I don't know why.'

Evonne stared at her lap, embarrassment stamped into every line of her figure, while Len Woodward glanced from her to Rick and back again, made his own, correct deductions, unbeknown to either of them, decided it was about time Rick Emerson had to fight for what he wanted, fond as he was of him—and remembered with an inward little sigh of nostalgia the good fight his wife had put up. Then he decided that if he was ever going to get this manuscript on the road he had better attempt to defuse this immediate situation.

'Well, that's sorted out,' he said genially. 'Funny thing, Rick, just a few days ago an advertising agency got in touch with me, asking for you. I think your Geography Department put them on to me.'

Rick raised an uninterested eyebrow.

'They're looking for an expert on Papua New Guinea, someone in touch with the local people, someone who would know the pitfalls for any advertising campaign up there.'

'There'd be plenty of those,' said Rick. 'I sometimes used to think no two of them spoke the same language!'

'But Pidgin is the sort of lingua franca, is it not?'

'Ah, Pidgin,' Rick drawled, but there was a sudden spark of curiosity in his eyes. 'What are they trying to sell?'

'I don't know. I think this is just the advance planning stage. In fact they're holding a two-day convention with the main theme being the marketing of Australian products outside Australia to our near neighbours—something like that. They wanted *you* to give a couple of talks.'

'Why the hell did they come to you?'

'I seemed to be the only person they could lay their hands on who had some idea of your whereabouts and availability,' Len Woodward said gently. 'I told them I doubted you'd be available, but one never quite knew. They said they'd live in hope until the last minute and keep a spot for you. Imagine my surprise when you rang me this morning, three days before our original appointment was scheduled . . .'

'Don't go on, Len,' Rick said wearily. 'I seem to be surrounded by people ramming my volatility and every other failing down my throat,' he added with a glance at Evonne. 'Anyway, why would I want to spend two days at a stuffy convention?'

'Stuffy? I don't know about that,' Len Woodward retorted. 'The opposite, I would have thought. They've certainly chosen a lovely spot for it. You know Peppers, don't you? Peppers at Pokolbin in the heart of the Hunter Valley?'

Rick had started to interject, but he went suddenly still and stared at his editor. Then he said slowly, 'Did you say Peppers? When?'

'Tomorrow and the next day. They expressly assured me they wouldn't expect you to spend all your time at the convention. Have you been to Peppers, Evonne?' Len Woodward turned to her suddenly.

Evonne blinked. 'I . . . no.'

'Never?'

'N-no,' she said uncertainly. 'Why . . . do you ask?'

'Marvellously peaceful spot for a bit of editing, that's all.'

The battle raged all the way up in the lift, for all that it was mostly silent—they weren't alone in the lift—but Evonne was saying to herself steadily, no, I will not, and communicating this fact with her eyes and her taut stance. Whereas Rick was suddenly almost relaxed, yet with a curiously devilish gleam in his eyes that frightened her.

They stepped out on the twenty-first floor, and Rick immediately took her hand and marshalled her implacably into his room, where he took up the attack in his own inimitable manner.

'You haven't lived until you've been to Peppers.'

'That's nonsense, and you know it!'

'I don't. You wait, there's something special about the place.'

'The most special place on *earth* is not going to change how I feel. I don't want to go anywhere with you. I'm beginning to be sorry I ever laid eyes on you...'

'Because I told you some home truths about yourself? Because any cauterising process is inevitably painful, because you've been dead from your beautiful neck down for a long time, like some citadel to a lost love, and I've managed to storm that citadel? Who was he, Evonne? I feel as if he ought to be written up in the *Guinness Book of Records*, such a man among men.' Rick folded his arms, leant his broad shoulders back against the door—they'd got no further than just inside the room—and waited impassively.

Evonne tightened her lips and turned her back on him.

'Tell me something else, then—are you packed?'

'*Yes!*'

'Good. So am I...once again we've read each other's minds.'

'No, we haven't. *I'm* going home.'

'Like an ostrich?' he said drily. 'Or do you really enjoy hurting yourself?'

Something in the way he said it made her turn slowly with a frown in her eyes. 'What . . .?' She stopped.

Rick stood upright. 'What do I mean?' he said softly. 'That you'd be far better going in the opposite direction, which Peppers is.'

'To what?' she whispered. 'Opposite to what? I don't know what you're talking about.'

'Don't you?' Rick smiled, but it didn't reach his eyes. 'I'm talking about Robert Randall, Evonne.'

CHAPTER SEVEN

FOR A moment Evonne thought she was going to faint. She swayed slightly and all the colour drained from her face, which Rick observed, but he made no move to touch or steady her.

'How...how?' she stammered, and put a hand to her throat.

'I consulted the oracle. On the phone. This morning,' he told her, then as her eyes widened in bewilderment he added impatiently, 'I rang my beloved uncle.'

She licked her lips. 'But he didn't know...'

'Didn't he? Perhaps you're right, but he gave it to me as his considered opinion. Incidentally, if you've wondered about it at all, that's why he sent you to me—that's why, in his opinion again, you consented to come on what must have seemed to you a mad mission. I believe there's some dinner on down there you would normally have attended, that the Randalls are attending.'

'He... Did you know any of this...before?'

'No. I would have thought that was obvious,' Rick said roughly. 'But it wasn't long before I began to suspect another lure. I doubt if even Uncle Amos expected it to be so successful,' he added grimly.

'Do you mean...do you...are you saying he threw us together for...to...' Evonne couldn't go on.

'Precisely. He decided you needed shaking out of your preoccupation with a man you couldn't have, and that I just might be the one to do it. He decided I needed the love of a good woman for a change.'

'I don't believe this,' Evonne said shakily, turning away again and groping her way towards a chair.

He followed. 'You wouldn't be contemplating going home for that dinner, would you? He has a *wife* and two children.'

'I *know* that.' Evonne stared blindly at her hands, twisting in her lap. 'No...'

'Then come to Peppers with me. What have you got to lose?'

Why she did just that, she didn't really know, except for the fact that she simply didn't seem to have the will to go on battering herself against him.

Nor the will to be surprised by or curious about anything much from then on. So that, when they were downstairs outside the main entrance, surrounded by their luggage, and an attendant brought a sleek blue Porsche to a halt opposite them and she realised it was Rick's, she merely blinked.

'I arranged to have it brought out of mothballs last week,' he explained as he nosed the car down the ramp, around and out into MacQuarie Street. 'Comfortable?'

Evonne nodded.

'I think we'll take the Putty Road. I know it's a bit winding, but the thought of negotiating the traffic through Hornsby doesn't appeal.'

'Whatever you like,' she shrugged.

'You don't care which road to hell we take, in other words?'

'Rick...' She said his name on a breath and put a hand to her mouth.

He glanced at her and said quietly then, 'Sorry.' He switched on the radio and didn't attempt any further conversation.

It was well past Windsor and deep into the Putty Road and the Blue Mountains that Evonne found herself feeling oddly guilty for her silence, for having sat so mute and miserable for the past couple of hours. She turned her head to look out of her side window, then raised her hand to massage the back of her neck. And slowly, the beauty of the scenery they were driving through got to her—the haze that even so close made the mountains blue, the white and yellow-barked huge gum trees beside the road, the banksias in the bush.

She said tentatively at last, 'It's lovely, isn't it?'

Rick nodded.

They flashed past a road sign. 'Do we go as far as Singleton?' she asked.

'No. We take the Broke turn-off. It's probably,' he shrugged, 'half an hour from there. Feeling better?'

'Yes.'

Once they were on the Broke turn-off, they were undoubtedly in vineyard country, and it was also beautiful, although different from the Putty Road, cleared and husbanded but still country, hilly but much gentler.

'Broke gets its name from these hills,' Rick told her. 'The Broken Back range.'

'Tell me about Peppers,' she invited.

'It's a guesthouse. It's designed in just about every respect to resemble an early Australian Colonial farmhouse, the décor inside as well as out, and it's run on guesthouse lines with all mod cons, discreetly disguised. It has a wonderful dining-room, beautiful grounds and gardens— and sometimes the air is like champagne. And it's situated amid some of the Hunter's best known wineries—Tyrrell's, Tulloch's, the Rothbury Estate, Hungerford Hill, Lindeman's— as well as a lot of smaller ones.'

'Like Moon Mountain,' Evonne suggested as they drove past the sign. 'What a lovely name!'

'Mmm. Not far now. There's Tyrrell's on our right.'

'Oh!' she exclaimed suddenly.

'What?'

'The roses! Did you see all those rose bushes up the drive?'

'We'll go back for a wine-tasting and a rose-viewing this afternoon if you like.' Rick turned the car off on to a side road to the right. 'And there, just up the hill, is Peppers.'

A few minutes later, as the Porsche coasted to a stop, Evonne stared around at Peppers, slumbering in the afternoon sunlight, and was unwittingly entranced. It comprised several buildings, all with creamy yellow walls and dark green corrugated iron roofs. Where they had stopped looked on to a courtyard and garden with wings on three sides, shaded walkways around it, white-painted sash windows in the upper storeys, and if you hadn't been told you would have thought you'd taken a step back in time.

'Is . . . is it new?' Evonne queried wonderingly.

Rick smiled at her. 'Wait until you see inside!'

But her delight in Peppers was tempered as she finally stood in the middle of a beautifully, authentically early-Colonial-decorated guest-room with an old-fashioned dressing-table and wardrobe, old prints and lithographs on the wall, a bowl of exquisite roses on the table, frilled pillowcases on the double bed—*their* room.

'You didn't tell me about this,' Evonne said jerkily.

'I didn't know they'd be fully booked, but,' Rick shrugged, 'it's what I had in mind anyway, so two rooms could have been a waste.'

'I can imagine!'

'Can you? Perhaps you can—you came with me, after all.'

Evonne sat down on the end of the bed. 'You said, when we left Brampton, there'd be no . . . there'd be no . . .'

'Coercion? There won't. There's also an extra bed.' He indicated the single divan that doubled as a settee with half a dozen plump little floral-covered cushions on it. 'You can always banish me to that, if you like,' he suggested with a sudden glint of amusement in his eyes.

'You're impossible, you know!'

'I know. Look, before you start to feel all tragic again, may I make a suggestion?'

Evonne shot him a fiery glance, but bit her lip on the retort that rose to mind. She wondered bleakly if she was being 'tragic'—a thought that made her wince. 'All right, make your suggestion,' she said coolly, however, and with the unspoken implication that it had better be good.

An hour later she had to admit to herself that it had been—the first part of his suggestion, at least.

'I see what you mean,' she said drowsily, from the yellow lounger she lay on, on the lawn in front of the pool-room which housed a sauna and spa, a heated indoor pool and the Pampering Place, where a masseuse offered massages, facials and other health and beauty treatments.

On the outdoor table between them and beneath a natural canvas and wooden umbrella, a bottle of wine raised its slender neck from a dewy silver ice bucket, two half-full wine-glasses stood, and the crumbs on a plate from the delicious smoked salmon sandwiches Rick had wangled from the kitchen because they had missed lunch.

'It is magic, isn't it?' Rick said quietly from his lounger.

'It's beautiful,' Evonne agreed, trailing her fingers on the lush green thick grass that was studded with flowering clover, and felt a desire to lie on it, to feel its rough texture on her body and the springiness of it beneath her weight. Above her the sky was blue and dotted with lazy clouds, and away to the east the ground fell away into a fold with some clumps of enormous ironbark gums and untouched bush, then gently rose again and was planted with vines in their serried rows. The only sounds to disturb the peace of the afternoon were the ying, y-i-n-g of a million cicadas in the bush, and the distant pop at irregular intervals of the air rifles used to frighten birds from the vines, and the only activity she could see was the occasional rise and fall of a tennis ball on the court that was on the other side of the grounds and down a slope.

'Where is everyone?' she asked. 'I feel almost as if we're the only two here on earth.'

Rick grinned. 'That's the other magic of Peppers—during the week, anyway. I think a lot of their weekday trade is in the form of conferences and conventions, so most of the other guests are probably tucked away in conference-rooms, working busily. Things might come alive tonight.'

Evonne reached for her wine-glass and sipped slowly. They both wore swimming costumes, she her emerald and black one, and it was hot. As usual she had smoothed on a sun-block, but, and perhaps more noticeably after the humidity of the Whitsundays and North Queensland, the air was dry and clear—it's like champagne, she thought.

'I suppose I ought to start telling you now,' she said after a while. 'Having been rendered soothed and almost comatose by the sun, the wine, the place.'

'Better than being overwrought,' Rick said quietly.

'And tragic,' she said drily.

'I'm sorry if that hurt...'

'No, don't be. The last thing I would want to be, and didn't realise I might have become, is any kind of a tragic figure. Funnily enough, there's not a great deal to tell.'

'About Robert Randall?'

'No. I... never slept with him. I... he didn't even know how I felt until...'

Rick sat up and reached over and put a hand on hers. 'Why don't you start at the beginning?'

'I've told you the beginning. We had similar experiences at the beginning, if you recall.'

'And there was nothing in between until Rob Randall hit your life?'

'Do you know him?' Evonne asked quickly, then bit her lip.

'I've met him. I know his wife's side of the family better—the Kingstons of Mirrabilla. I once—for a short period—went to the same school as Ian Kingston, although he was three years ahead of me. He was killed in a plane crash. And we were once invited to Mirrabilla where I met Clarissa Kingston... who's now Mrs Robert Randall, I believe.'

Evonne closed her eyes. 'Yes.'

'But go on—were you a multi-affaired person in the interim?'

Evonne's lashes flew up. 'I wouldn't *dream* of asking you a question like that!'

'That's the difference between us, Patterson,' said Rick with his lips quirking. 'But one day, perhaps, you'll be possessed of the same curiosity.'

Evonne compressed her lips, then thought with sudden exasperation, why not tell him everything? I might get some peace if I do. 'Twice-affaired—does that make me multi?' she queried ironically.

'A total of three in all those years? No, I'd hardly say so,' he drawled.

'Thank you,' she replied grimly.

'Were they worthwhile?'

'No, they were not,' she said precisely. 'The first one was—I thought—another love of my life but again I got the brush-off, although,' she paused, 'he didn't leave me quite empty-handed. It was also a business relationship, and instead of the proverbial diamond bracelet I got a promotion. So I finally got myself together, and said to myself, well, bingo! I'm getting the hang of this...' She stopped and sighed and drank some more wine. 'The next time, I wasn't even surprised. And in exchange for another small step up the ladder, I made no fuss, no scenes, but...' She stopped again and this time didn't go on.

Until Rick said, 'I know the feeling.'

Evonne turned her head to him. 'Do you? I don't think you could possibly...'

'Cynicism can come to anyone, man or woman.'

'Cynical—well, yes, I was that,' she conceded wearily. 'But it was more—it was the knowledge that I hadn't changed. I still had the same lousy judgement, I still...was too intense, too ready to believe I was in love—the most dangerous person that existed for me *was* me. So I decided I'd get my promotions and diamond bracelets...'

she broke off and smiled a little bitterly, 'I was going to say the hard way, but whatever, on my feet, not my back.'

Rick smiled slightly.

Evonne laid her head back. 'It was a real coup to get...to get the job at Randalls.'

'And you fell in love with him.'

'Yes.'

'You said he didn't even know?'

Evonne closed her eyes again. 'No...until I had to tell him.' The sun was warm on her eyelids.

'How did you keep him from knowing—until then?'

'I don't know,' she said after a long time. 'It wasn't easy, but I suppose he wasn't looking for it. He had...you see, he had a girl in his heart, who also happened to be his wife, but she was very young then, Clarissa...Clarry, but, more than young, I think she was very innocent, yet things weren't right between them. I...' her voice shook a little, 'became a friend of hers, which was the last thing I wanted or believed could happen. She was everything I wasn't and desperately wanted to be, and I resented her bitterly for that as well as for—him. But I couldn't resist her warmth and her innate grace...she was that kind of person. She was also naïve and trusting, and owing to circumstances I couldn't control we got really close. At one stage I became *her* secretary-stroke-companion, as she used to call it, and I stayed at Mirrabilla and helped her...she'd never taken any part in his social life, the social part of his business life at least, and she was very nervous about it.'

Rick waited.

'Then one day she found out how I felt about him. I...unwittingly I gave myself away completely, and because...because of the difficulties of *their* relationship, she thought it was reciprocal and I couldn't make her believe it wasn't, I couldn't get through to her at all. I also knew it was a crisis time in their marriage for other reasons, so...' Evonne broke off and opened her eyes, 'I had to go and tell him what had happened, how I felt about him, how I'd given myself away to Clarry...without even knowing she was *there* at the time...how she wouldn't listen and believed he felt the same way about me. It was the only thing I could do.'

This time as the silence stretched even the cicadas took a breathing space. 'She was,' Evonne said finally, 'the only other girl I ever got close to.'

'And you still, in your heart, feel you betrayed her?'

She sighed. 'Yes. But it didn't stop me loving him, although I left him—I mean, I resigned there and then and I've never seen him since, except once. I saw them both once, and from the way they were I couldn't doubt she'd...finally grown up for him. There,' she passed a hand over her eyes, but they were dry, 'now you know the whole sad story, and all about me.' She smiled wryly. 'It all sounded rather trite and...much ado about nothing, didn't it?'

'Except that you acted honourably. Perhaps you have more innate grace than you realise, Evonne.'

'Yes—I acted honourably,' she agreed. 'In the end. I should never have let it get to that stage, though. I should have gone away from the moment I realised what was happening to me. Somehow, I just couldn't.'

'And you haven't been able to forget him?'

She stared at the horizon unseeingly and said nothing.

'Well,' Rick sat back, 'unfortunately or fortunately, we can't all be Robert Randalls—I certainly can't offer you the kind of empire he has, but I do have one thing he hasn't got.'

Evonne sat up and refilled her wine-glass. 'You don't have to. I'm not feeling sorry for myself, or tragic, so you don't have to jolt me out of it or offer any wise palliatives, or insults, for that matter—in fact, I'd rather you didn't say another word on the subject. Let's just forget it—you wanted to know, now you do.'

'I was merely about to point out something you don't seem to know about *me*, something I normally don't trade on, in fact it's often a darn nuisance, but . . . my psyche appears to be a bit bruised,' Rick admitted.

'Your what?' she queried.

'My ego,' he repeated, and there was a wicked little glint in his eyes. 'So, in the context of trying to measure up to Robert Randall, I thought I might tell you I am, as well as everything else I am, a baronet. Someone was bound to mention it eventually.'

Evonne had been sipping her wine and she choked suddenly. 'You're joking!' she spluttered, but almost immediately remembered Basil

Brush, and a few other little things such as the speculative look in his eye when she had once called Rick *Mr* Emerson, the confusion on Brampton when she'd *asked* for Mr Emerson . . .

'Oh, to be honest, I've done nothing to earn it, one merely has to be one's father's son, but I did actually see myself once described as being eminently eligible on account of it.' Rick raised his eyebrows. 'And of course my looks. There's an elderly estate in England that goes with it . . . it always rather annoyed my father before he died that I seemed to prefer Australia, but after all, my mother was an Australian. How am I doing now, in your estimation?'

Evonne stared at him, then started to laugh softly. 'You're . . .' She couldn't go on for a moment as the laughter shook her from head to toe, but finally she did say, 'Sir Richard, you're wonderful, I don't think I've ever met anyone quite like you!'

He grinned and stretched out a hand to her again. 'I love you when you laugh. Come and have a spa with me and then a swim.'

She sobered. 'I didn't mean . . .'

'I know you didn't—it's all right, I only wanted to change the mood. I also thought it might embarrass you if someone else told you.'

'Just wait until I get my hands on your uncle Amos!' Evonne exclaimed indignantly.

During their spa and swim, it occurred to Evonne that she felt curiously like a prisoner set free, oddly lighthearted, although nothing had changed. She was still the same person with the same problems—and she was sharing a room with her current main problem. What am I going to do about him? she wondered. What's he going to spring on me next? I don't have to be a genius to know . . . surely the magic of Peppers isn't so powerful as to make me not even care? Yet I seem to be emotionally wrung out, dangerously detached from myself.

They left the spa and she became detached even from her thoughts as they plunged into the pool.

She rose to the surface, gasping. 'If this is heated, I'd hate to feel it when it isn't!'

'I think they rely on solar power in the summer,' said Rick, pointing to the clear plastic panels in the roof. 'I promise you you'll feel marvellous afterwards, though.'

Something slipped through her detachment as they returned to the room to get ready for dinner. She stood twisting her towel, feeling awkward and, because of it, irritated. She hadn't unpacked, neither had Rick, and suddenly she knew it was an impossible situation, overwhelming, fencing her in.

'Tell you what,' he said, with an oddly alert little look at her expression, 'why don't I shower and dress first and then clear out and leave you to it? I'll take the opportunity to make myself known to this advertising mob. You could meet me in the bar when you're ready. I've booked a table for dinner at seven-thirty.'

Evonne considered, then nodded, and within a remarkably short time she had the room to herself. She sat down on the bed for a few minutes, then with a sigh got up and unpacked a few things, and got ready herself.

She was still in a quiet, thoughtful mood as she made her way to the bar, stopping frequently to admire and touch some of the lovely things with which Peppers abounded—beautiful old tables, lamps, paintings, china vases and plates on stands from a bygone era, one particularly exquisite little plate painted with violets, the wooden floors and old rugs.

Rick was sitting on a bar stool talking energetically to a man, but although Evonne stopped a few feet away and behind him, he turned his head suddenly and stood up with a hand outstretched to her.

She hesitated as his gaze rested on her, taking in the simple cool carnation-pink voile dress, her loose hair and bare legs, her pink high-heeled sandals, her gold bracelet and string of small, perfectly matched pearls, her glossy pink lips, her eyes which were suddenly so uncertain...

Then the moment broke and she moved forward, but from then on, the evening—the events, the people she was introduced to—everything took on a curiously blurred outline.

She said little, and was dimly relieved when Rick dexterously avoided an invitation to dine with the fifteen or so advertising agency people gathered for the conference due to get under way the next day. She took in a vague impression of the charm of the dining-room—huge old dressers, dark bluey-green walls, pink floral tablecloths. She ate deliciously sweet grilled scampi, and pearl perch for the main course as the late daylight of eastern summertime faded and the lawns and creepers beyond the dining-room windows became shadows.

She said, out of the blue and apropos of nothing to Rick, 'How did you know I was there? In the bar?'

'Some sixth sense.' His green eyes held hers until she looked away.

And when finally he suggested they have their coffee on the veranda, she acquiesced.

There was a moon rising and silvering the sweep of lawn below, the rose bushes and, beyond, the surface of a small dam.

'I knew there'd be a moon,' she whispered, holding her coffee-cup in both hands, then putting it down carefully because her hands were shaking.

'Evonne?'

But she wouldn't, couldn't look at him—there were tears in her eyes anyway, as she said, 'I have to be honest—I dressed for you,' she fingered the carnation-pink voile, 'I wanted to be young and...carefree for you, but I can't. I didn't even realise what I was doing, feeling, until you turned and looked at me in the bar. I thought...I'd even thought you were hemming me in. Now I know...' She stopped helplessly.

'You want to be—hemmed in?' Rick said quietly.

'I couldn't bear to be alone tonight,' she said starkly. 'That's the only thing I *know*. And it wouldn't be fair to tell you any different. I'm sorry.'

He was silent for so long, she felt a trembling begin within her, a desire to take back her words, to shape them differently, to explain better, but how could she explain better what she didn't understand herself? How could she tell him she was vulnerable as much to the moonlight, the scent of roses, the place, her *senses*, as to him? Tell him that she didn't understand how this could have happened to her, that it was shaming, but out of nowhere, a pit of loneliness so deep yawned at her feet that she was in real, dire fear.

She moved, went to get up awkwardly, horrified suddenly as well as afraid, horrified at the insult she had offered him in the name of honesty and her preoccupation with herself.

'Where are you going, Evonne?'

She sank back and forced herself to look at him at last, but so afraid of what she might see. 'I shouldn't have said that,' she stammered, and flinched visibly at his shuttered, carved expression. 'It was unforgivable...' Her agitated words sank into a pool of silence and her heart started to beat heavily as Rick's lips twisted into a dry little smile.

'All the same, it's just as well I'm available, isn't it?' he drawled.

'Rick,' she whispered, 'I...'

But his eyes were alive suddenly, she saw, alive and green and supremely mocking—then, in a lightning change, frighteningly inscrutable and like a tiger's, she thought chaotically, delaying, playing...oh, what have I done?

In a purely reflex action she glanced around wildly, but that only brought another absent little smile to his lips. 'You're quite free to run away, my dear,' he said softly, 'but I'm going back to our room.' He stood up and stared down at her, and the implication that she was a coward was quite plain, as was the challenge.

She bent her head, her hair fell forward and her shoulders sagged. Then she stood up herself.

CHAPTER EIGHT

Rick unlocked the door of their room, put a hand in to switch on the light, then stood aside for her.

Evonne went in and he closed the door behind them—she watched him close it and lock it by pressing the knob in on the round brass handle. She watched him lay the key on the writing-table, flick on a lamp beside the bed and turn off the overhead light, then go to each of the sash windows, lowering them as far as they would go.

Then he turned his attention to her.

She was standing across the room from him, her hands at her sides, her foolish tears dried up, her eyes bleak.

He said, barely audibly, 'Come here, Evonne.'

'Rick, I...'

'Damn you,' he said, so softly but with an edge of violence that made her shiver, 'don't make me come and get you. But that's what you want, isn't it? So that then you can curse me in your most colourful language, and fight...and be subdued. That's how you like it, don't you? Rough. How could I have forgotten?' he mocked.

'Oh...no, no, I don't,' she whispered, shivering uncontrollably now.

'Then you like putting the responsibility for *wanting* it everywhere but on yourself.'

'You don't understand…' She stopped and her eyes widened suddenly as at last she *did* begin to slowly see through to her inner self.

'Tell me what I don't understand, then,' he said with irony and insolent patience. 'Just don't give me that old line about loneliness again,' he warned savagely.

Evonne swallowed and licked her lips, then her eyes lit with a spark of anger that she should have brought herself to this, that *he* should have. 'I'm scared stiff, if you must know,' she said, and thought her voice sounded curiously hollow. 'It's been years, for one thing,' she turned away convulsively but went on with her hand to her mouth, 'and I've only ever been a failure anyway. There must be…secret sophistications I've never learnt, rough——' her voice broke, but she went on hoarsely '—talking about that—edges, things I don't know how to control—myself, for example… I warned you once before, but you wouldn't listen.' And she covered her face with her hands and ground her teeth in despair.

'Evonne…' Rick said her name from across the room.

'If only you'd stuck to Patterson!'

He was beside her in a couple of strides, swinging her around to face him, his hands hard on her upper arms. 'Don't! You're wrong…'

'No, I'm not wrong, *Sir* Richard.' New tears streamed down her face and she wrested a wrist free and scrubbed at her eyes, but that wrecked her mascara and when she saw it on her fingers, she laughed as well as cried. Laughed as she said,

'Of all people, *you* know about the tough, brash side of me.'

He closed his eyes briefly. 'Stop it,' he commanded softly.

But she couldn't. 'Perhaps you don't know...how I heard myself talked about once, but I'll tell you... "A piece of hot stuff, but she'd wear you out before you're forty"...that's what someone I barely knew said, and he went on to say he'd got it by word of mouth from a man— a man I did know and thought I'd loved. Do you know how I felt? Like a tart, as if that's how I'd been.'

'Oh, Evonne!' Rick muttered beneath his breath, and drew her, sobbing uncontrollably now against him, and cupped the back of her head in his hand and laid his cheek on her hair.

They stayed like that for a long time until her storm of weeping subsided into the odd ragged, hiccupy breath, and she mumbled, 'Sorry...I'm all right now. I did tell you this might not be a good idea.'

She heard him sigh, then he said, 'Come,' and released her but took her hand and led her to the bed. 'Lie down,' he ordered, and when she sat down, he pulled up the pillows and bent down to take off her shoes. Then he disappeared into the bathroom and when he came back with a glass of water and some tissues she'd curled up against the pillows.

But she sat up and sipped the water gratefully, then blew her nose and wiped her eyes, grimacing at the streaks on the tissues, black combined with her silvery blue eye-shadow and pink blusher. 'I must look awful,' she sighed with a sketchy attempt at a smile. 'This make-up obviously isn't as waterproof as it claims!' She laid her head back and fought some more weak tears.

'Evonne,' Rick took the glass out of her fingers and set it down, then he lay down beside her, not touching but facing her, his head propped on his arm.

She sniffed, then lowered her gaze from the ceiling to look into his eyes. 'I really am sorry to... to have burdened you with the mess I am. You'd think, at twenty-eight, one would have sorted oneself out a bit better. Fancy,' she marvelled, and plucked at the pink voile of her dress, 'even trying to be the girl I probably never was!'

He caught her fingers in a firm grip. 'Will you let me show you the real Evonne Patterson? The person *I* know she is. The one who's made her mistakes—but then we all do that, don't ever for one minute think you're the only one.'

'Why is it different for me, then?'

'Because you've got a chip on your shoulder, Evonne,' he said honestly. 'You're also bright, brighter than most, more *alive* until you decided to die in a way, and you've fought against enormous odds. But there's one thing you should never regret... if you're loving and passionate, and if when you love, even mistakenly, you give it your all, don't regret it. There also has to be someone to match you, someone who'll love the sheer magnificence of you.'

She closed her eyes and her lashes were wet on her cheeks.

'Did you ever stop to think that what you felt for Rob Randall might have grown out of proportion because he didn't want you?'

'Reverse psychology?' she said twistedly.

'It might have put him, in your mind, a cut above the ones who did.'

She sighed a shuddering little sigh. 'Perhaps.'

'Then,' his green eyes glinted suddenly, 'what are we going to do about this bloke lying next to you? What category shall we put him in? Because I can't deny he wants you, rather desperately. On the other hand, he has no diamond bracelets in mind for you or steps up any ladder, and there are times when, I have to confess, he feels like strangling you—he's in a bad way, I'm afraid.'

'Oh, Rick!' she breathed, and touched his hair, picked up a bright sun-streaked strand and felt its texture between her fingers, then slid her hand down the side of his face, 'you're so sweet when you're not wanting to strangle me!'

'In that context,' his eyes were wry, 'may I kiss you?'

'Well...'

But she got no further, because that was when he suited words to action.

'Oh, help me...'

Rick lifted his head from her breasts. 'I'll do anything you want me to. I'm in need of some help myself.'

'Tell me,' Evonne whispered.

He transferred his lips to her throat and she felt him laugh softly. 'It's just that I can't wait much longer.'

'Don't, then.'

'Are you sure?'

Her answer was a low husky sound of desire.

'If I'm hurting you, tell me . . .'

'I don't think anything has hurt me less—for someone with a left-handed syndrome, you're remarkably deft.'

'If I am it's because you're incredibly beautiful,' he said with an effort, and eased his weight on to her. 'I'm sorry—I meant to take much longer about this.'

'Any longer and I might die—we seem to be talking a lot,' Evonne whispered innocently.

'I always talk a lot, hadn't you noticed? But I shall desist if . . .'

'No,' she slipped her arms around his back and stroked the strong length of it, 'keep talking to me, please . . . oh . . .' She stopped as he eased her legs apart with his.

And from somewhere he found the control to keep talking to her in between kissing her again and simply holding her and touching her until her reflex shrinking had subsided, because he had known better than she that the long, lonely years needed time to bridge. And at last she was truly ready to welcome him with a pleading little gasp. 'Oh, please, yes!'

At last he gave way to the hard, driving force he had controlled, and she moaned and clung to him, arched her body to his to meet it, to match it, to be possessed by the thrusting rhythm, to be suddenly slippery with sweat but uncaring, to give herself to him totally, her legs twined around his, her hands in his hair, to be strong and proud of it. Until that wave upon wave of sensation caught her in its grip and she was no longer strong but supremely vulnerable, completely at his mercy, saying his name over and over in her throat.

Rick held her in silence for a long time after he had rolled away from her, held her as she wept quietly from pure reaction, and his own heavy breathing subsided. Then at last he smoothed her hair away from her face and kissed her brow. 'Evonne?'

'Mmm...' It was all she could manage.

'Words fail me...I just thought I ought to tell you that.'

'Me too,' she whispered shakily. 'No, they don't. Thank you,' she said simply.

He gathered her close. 'Can you sleep if I hold you like this? I don't seem to be willing or able to let you go—that's the problem.'

'I don't think I can sleep any other way.' She smiled tremulously at him, their faces only inches apart on the pillow.

'Good, because...' But she stopped him with a finger to his lips, then moved slightly to kiss his lips.

'If you're going to talk to me all night, though...'

He laughed, and she caught her breath and felt something like a hand squeezing her heart with the foreknowledge that she could only banter like this because the alternative was to tell him what she really felt. The love growing in her heart... No, no, she thought with a little flare of panic, don't make that mistake again even with Rick, perhaps especially with Rick. Go on teasing him, anything, but not that...

Because it was dark with only the moonlight to see by, Rick couldn't see what was in her eyes, she hoped, and anyway, it was as if they had suddenly both run out of small talk, because he pulled her even closer so her head rested on his shoulder, and he stroked her hair gently until, unknowingly, she fell asleep.

What she didn't know, either, was that it was some time before he followed suit.

She woke before he did and blinked at the sunlight flooding the room. Her watch told her it was eight-thirty, but her body told her something else—that she had no desire to leave the rumpled bed, although she drew the sheet modestly up around her, and turned to lie with her cheek on her hand and drink her fill of Rick Emerson as he slept.

Once she even put her hand out to touch his long, golden body, but she stopped herself. And her heart beat a little tattoo as he stirred, groaned and sat up, pushing a hand through his hair and staring around as if he had not the slightest idea where he was. Then his eyes rested on her and widened with relief, and he lay back with another groan and pulled her into his arms. 'I thought I'd dreamt it,' he mumbled, burying his face in her hair.

'Oh, Rick,' she whispered, a smile trembling on her lips.

Then, about five minutes later, he said, 'What's the time?'

'About a quarter to nine.'

'Bloody *hell*!' He released her and sat up again, rubbing his face distractedly.

'What?' she queried.

'I'm supposed to be delivering the opening address at this bloody conference at half past nine... I haven't the faintest idea what I'm going to say, I'm supposed to talk for an *hour*—how do I get myself *into* these bl...'

'Shh!' Evonne sat up and picked up his hand. 'No more swearing, it's bad first thing in the morning. I'll help you.'

'How?' he demanded.

'Well,' she considered, 'while you get ready and have breakfast, I'll make the rough outline of a speech for you. I'm good at that, it even used to be my job—and,' she went on serenely as he shot her a glance, 'what about something to do with the trials and tribulations of Pidgin? Of which, since typing up your book, I have some knowledge now. I can even think of a good title— something like, say... *Belong what name you fight 'im dis fellow police boy?* At least with an outline—well, especially for you, you'd have no trouble filling in the rest.'

Rick stared at her, at her bare shoulders, at the sheet she was still wearing modestly, then he lifted a hand and pulled it away and her breasts were exposed, satiny and threaded with pale blue veins beneath the gloss of her white skin, fuller than it appeared when she was dressed, tipped with velvet. And he said something beneath his breath, and once again lay down, taking her with him. 'I can't,' he said.

'Yes, you can. You have to—they might come looking for you.'

He started to swear even more comprehensively until he realised she was laughing silently. Then he grinned too, at last, and relaxed.

But after a minute or so he said, 'I'll go, if I can ask you a question—and get an honest answer.' He took her chin in one hand.

Her lashes fluttered, but she said, 'Go ahead.'

'Belong what name you really feel dis morning?'

Evonne thought, then said gravely, 'Pretty damn good! Belong dis name.'

Years of long practice, she guessed, saw Rick shower, shave and dress in no time at all, as she sat in bed with a pen and pad, thinking briefly, then, from the top of her head, which she was good at, starting to write swiftly.

He went to breakfast and returned at twenty-five past nine with a tray, by which time she had covered several pages with her smooth, flowing script.

She looked up. 'What's this?'

'Breakfast for you. It finishes at nine-thirty, so I told them you weren't feeling well.'

Evonne looked at the tray, which bore fruit, a selection of cold meat and cheese, a croissant and coffee, and one raggedly plucked, perfect pink rosebud. 'Thanks,' she said huskily, and handed him the pad. 'See what you make of that.'

Rick scanned the pages swiftly, then looked at her with genuine admiration in his eyes. 'This is perfect—better than anything I could have come up with.'

'I doubt that, and you'll still have to ad-lib a bit—something you excel at,' she told him with a twinkle in her eye.

He grinned. 'If only I had you to organise my work on a permanent basis! I'm gone,' he added, and kissed her briefly, 'but like you and General MacArthur, I too shall return.'

During the morning, Evonne made a conscious effort to analyse her state of mind. She also took Rick's manuscript to the lawn outside the pool-room with the intention of doing some editing, but found she couldn't concentrate—on any-thing. So she had a spa bath and found the buf-feting of the water on her body soothing, then a swim which was bracing. Now I'll really be able to think, she thought as she climbed out of the pool—and proved herself correct as, through the glass doors, she saw Rick approaching across the grass.

He had changed into shorts and a T-shirt, he had his old straw hat tilted low over his eyes, and he stopped at the table where his manuscript lay, studied it for a moment, then looked around for her.

Evonne stood transfixed with memories of their lovemaking flooding her mind—and dis-covered, in that instant, the exact state of her mind. All that had lain dormant within her rose to the surface and she found herself trembling like a girl, thinking—oh, what shall I do with myself?—conscious only of Rick, his hands and mouth, the way his hair grew, remembering the strength of his legs, drowning in his nearness . . .

Then he turned and saw her and she moved jerkily to pick up her towel, and used it not only to dry herself but hide her emotions.

'There you are,' he said, sliding the screen door back. 'I've escaped.'

'How did it go?'

'Oh, I slayed 'em!'

'You're incurably modest,' Evonne remarked.

'Thanks to you—I was about to add, but I got sidetracked.' He stared at her.

'I didn't notice...Rick, not...someone will see us.'

'No, they won't,' he said softly, and drew her cool, fresh body into his arms.

'I'm...I'm still wet,' she protested.

'A gorgeous wet mermaid, a siren, enticing men to their doom,' he said, his lips barely moving and his eyes glinting. 'I shall have to do one of two things.'

'Let me go before I make your clothes all damp?' Evonne offered.

'If we do one of the things I have in mind, it won't matter in the slightest—I'd have to take my clothes off anyway. The other,' he wound her wet hair into a rope around one hand, 'is more practical. Care to come for a spin, a spot of wine-tasting and lunch? You choose.'

'The latter,' she said promptly. 'Let's be practical.' But as she said the words she knew she was fighting her desire to do the former.

Rick's lips twisted wryly. 'It will only be prolonging the agony,' he warned.

Her gaze softened. 'We can be close mentally, though.'

He looked at her intently for a moment, then he said gently, 'How lovely that sounds!' He released her but took her hand and kissed her fingers.

Everything they did from then on assumed, for Evonne, a new dimension. Not only what they did, but every object seemed to stand out more clearly for her, the very sky seemed bluer and the grass greener.

They started out at Tyrrell's Winery, tasted some, then wandered through the dim cool rooms inhabited by silent round wooden casks each with a dash of whitewash on the earth floor beneath its tap.

'To show whether they're leaking?' she suggested.

'Obviously,' Rick said ruefully. 'Why didn't I think of that?'

'I have the more practical mind, that's all,' she said, and they laughed together as he put his arm round her shoulders.

Then they visited two smaller, newer wineries, with impressive, freshly decorated wine-tasting halls but not the atmosphere of the older ones.

'I like old things,' said Evonne dreamily.

'Then you'll like Tulloch's, our next stop, and that's where we'll have lunch.'

'I'm glad about that—lunch, I mean.'

'I know what you mean—they may be only little glasses, but they add up.'

Tulloch's really satisfied her soul, she told him. It was peaceful, set amid trees, an old white building with tables and benches outside to eat at. Instead of the restaurant she had expected, there was a small shop, the Champagne Sandwich Shop, and the sandwiches were freshly made, special and delicious. Evonne chose turkey fillings, and they took them and their drinks outside and sat eating and drinking slowly and listening to the birds in the trees. She told Rick about her passion for Australiana, and they talked as they had never really done before.

Back in the car they fell silent, though mentally united in a way she realised her soul had hungered for for so long, and it was awesome— and frightening.

Back at Peppers Rick told her with regret that he had to go back to the conference for the last session of the day—a question-time-like session, apparently.

'It's all right,' she said softly.

'What will you do?'

'Indulge my other passion,' she told him, then bit her lip.

He stared into her eyes. 'Don't take it back,' he said very quietly.

'Rick,' she whispered.

But he put a finger to her lips. 'Tell me about this other one.'

'Down the road,' she said after a moment, 'in the middle of nowhere really, there's this antique shop.'

'Ah. Yes, it's new—since the last time I was here, anyway. Would you like the car?'

'No, it's not far to walk. It will do me good.'

'Don't stray too far,' he said, and kissed her lingeringly.

It was a few minutes after he had disappeared before Evonne collected herself sufficiently to go anywhere.

The owners of the antique shop lived on the premises in a beautiful stone house, and after a satisfying look through their wares she bought an old silver butter dish for her mother, and stopped to chat to the owners, who she discovered had recently gone into winemaking. And she bought a bottle of their first vintage, a Peppers Creek Semillion Chardonnay, for Rick.

She wandered back up the hill to Peppers in the late afternoon sunlight, breathing in the scent of grass, revelling in the peace and beauty of the countryside, unable to pierce the serenity of her mood.

Rick had not returned when she got back to their room, and she lay down just to relax for a while, and fell asleep.

She woke to find him leaning over her.

'Oh . . . you're back,' she mumbled.

'Mmm . . . and you're exquisite, even in sleep.'

Evonne smiled drowsily and he lay down beside her.

'Did you slay them again?' she asked with her head on his shoulder, her fingers fiddling with the buttons of his shirt.

'I'm afraid so,' he replied gloomily.

'You don't seem happy about it,' she remarked after a moment.

'I'm not,' he said, between kissing her brow and stroking her hair behind her ear. 'They liked me so much, they've organised a dinner in my honour tonight. I really couldn't find a way to get out of it.'

Evonne's lips twitched, but she said gravely, 'The penalty for such popularity.'

'You're invited too...of course. Will you mind very much?'

'Oh—well, one does have to eat, I guess,' she said reservedly.

He held her away and looked into her eyes. 'You're laughing at me,' he accused reproachfully.

And she was, although she hid her face in his shoulder, but he could feel it shaking her body.

'Am I such a clown?' he asked wryly after a moment.

'No—right now you're my own beautiful, most improbable lecturer, geographer and baronet, that's all. Don't change a hair of your head,' she advised, lifting her face to him, still laughing tenderly.

Rick caught his breath. 'And you're...oh, *damn*!' he said exasperatedly, falling back against the pillows.

'What now?' she whispered, a new smile curving her lips.

'We've only got half an hour, that's what!'

'Half an hour now, but all night later. These things shouldn't be rushed, should they?'

'No, mama,' he said meekly but with a devilish little glint in his eyes.

'Perhaps we should both take a cold shower?' she suggested.

'Even the coldest shower, if we took it together,' he said meditatively, 'couldn't hope to combat certain co-habitual concerns you arouse in me.'

'You ran out of Cs!'

He grinned. 'Care to contribute a couple?'

Evonne thought for a moment. 'Considering the congruent course of our concupiscence—beat that one if you can!'

'I'm not even sure what it *means*!'

'Considering it anyway, could I...could I have my shower first?'

'Oh, I think concupiscence earns you that honour, Miss Patterson.' He released her with a flourish but almost immediately pulled her back into his arms and kissed her soundly. 'The loser's spoils,' he said softly and wickedly. 'Off you go.'

Evonne thought while she dressed for dinner how different this evening was from the last, how they shared the bathroom mirror, how Rick did up the zip at the back of her saffron Thai silk dress, how he watched her stand in front of the dressing-table and put on a pair of gold and black-rimmed pearl ear-rings and her watch, then, as the last touch to her preparations, spray some perfume to the base of her throat.

'There!' she said, turning to him. 'Will I do?'

He brushed a hand through his hair and straightened. He had been leaning against the bathroom doorway, and in true Rick style he wore his check jacket over a collarless shirt. His hair needs a trim, she thought, and really, for who he is, he does need more formal clothes.

'You'll do,' he interrupted her thoughts. 'Won't I?'

'I...did I say something?'

'You looked it. As if you were about to start inspecting my ears!'

Evonne smiled ruefully. 'Sorry.'

'Come here,' he said softly. She moved towards him, but he only took her hand. 'Does it worry you that I'm one of those thoroughly disorganised people?'

Her lips parted in surprise and she wondered if he could read her mind. 'No,' she said after a slight hesitation.

'Tell me if it does. I'll try to reform.'

'Rick, this is an odd conversation to start now!'

'From now on I'll start hanging up my clothes!'

'I wouldn't here—this isn't your kind of hotel in that respect,' she told him. 'Shall we go? We're ten minutes late already.'

He stared into her eyes and his were curiously sombre for an instant, she thought. Then a slow smile crept into them. 'All right, we'll leave it for now,' he drawled. 'What do they say about the attraction of opposites?'

A flicker of uncertainty crossed Evonne's face and a frisson contracted her nerves. 'I'm not sure,' she said huskily. 'What do they say?'

Rick shrugged and let go of her hand. 'Just that it's eminently possible. Sometimes they even supply a crying need in each other. Remember that.'

'Rick...' she took a breath, 'don't...'

But he put his arm around her. 'Stay by my side tonight—I'll get incredibly lonely otherwise. And would you do something else?'

She stared up at him. 'What?'

'Smile for me now. Just for me.'

Her lips trembled, then she did, and he closed his eyes briefly and hugged her hard, then let her go with a twisted smile of his own. 'Sorry if I've mussed you up.'

'I don't think you have,' she said breathlessly.

But later he 'mussed her up' considerably!

It was a pleasant dinner, and with her advertising background Evonne was able to hold her end up, as she thought of it, fairly well. If she was distracted she thought she alone was aware of it. It was harder to put a name to the cause of her distraction, then she realised it stemmed from what Rick had said about the differences between them, what she had been thinking about him—and that was when her distraction hardened into clear thought. Could it ever work? she thought. How *could* it—we're so different, and only fools believe love conquers all. Which means—oh, but why be blind, Evonne? Haven't you learnt anything?

The party moved to the veranda for coffee, where she was struck by another revelation. Despite his best efforts, Rick had been parted from her. He did not, outwardly at least, appear bereft as he sat between two attractive women, laughing and talking. But as she watched she could see their subtle admiration, their extra animation and the ease with which he handled it, and she experienced a stirring of pure jealousy that shook her to the core. And she sipped her coffee and thought, so, it's happened to me again, only this time I'll not stay to the bitter end. One more night...that's all I'll allow myself. One more night.

'Penny for 'em?'

She jumped and looked into Rick's oddly intent green eyes. 'Oh! I...I was miles away,' she stammered.

'So I saw. I'm going to make our excuses and leave now. I think we've done our duty. Coming?'

'Yes...Yes,' she said disjointedly, putting her cup down and standing up.

He was charming and gracious but deaf to all protests that the night was still young. 'Thank you all very much, but I really need my sleep.'

And when the senior member of the party looked set to make a speech, Rick forestalled him with a grin and a murmured, 'It was really my pleasure. If you need any more information, just contact me, I'll be delighted to help. Goodnight, everyone!' And with a wave he drew Evonne off the veranda and on to the lawn and round a corner of the building out of sight. Whereupon he took her in his arms, kissed her urgently and said, 'Let's get away from here.'

They took the long way round, across the east lawn, and stopped to admire the moon.

'Oh, look at that plane,' said Evonne, and pointed to the twinkling lights. 'It's on a flight path across the moon.'

'So am I,' Rick murmured, and drew her gently into the shadows of the pool-room veranda, which was closed and darkened for the night. 'Do you know, I've been plagued by this fantasy of making love to you out there on the grass, preferably in the sunlight, but moonlight wouldn't be a bad alternative.'

'Rick,' she breathed, leaning back against the wall as he started to kiss her again, 'we couldn't!'

'I know—don't look so scared! But don't you think it would be lovely lying in it together, getting it in our hair... getting carried away? Would you care if I pushed your skirt above your hips and slipped your...'

'Don't,' she whispered shakily.

'But would you?' he said against the corner of her mouth.

'No... what am I saying?' Her voice caught in her throat, but it was too late, she was drowning helplessly in desire fuelled by his hands on her, the feel of him, his wandering lips. She thought dimly that she had never felt so sensuously alive yet curiously weak, with a flame of longing running through her body. She thought, as Rick pressed her to the wall, that if he didn't stop soon she would lie in the grass with him exactly as he wished. She said despairingly, 'How do you do this to me?'

'Tell me what I do to you.'

'It's as if...it's never happened before. It's like being a young girl and...the first time. I keep thinking...what will I do with myself? What...how did this happen?' she whispered with almost incredulous confusion.

He slid both hands up her throat and cupped her face. 'I could tell you, but would you believe me?'

'No, not that... I *can't*!' she stared up in anguish into his eyes.

He released her face but took her into his arms until her trembling had subsided. 'One day at a time, then,' he said softly. 'Let's just take one day at a time. Will you let me take you to our room and make love to you as if we were out here?'

Evonne didn't reply, she could only cling to him.

He did just that.

He laid her on the bed and slid her skirt up above her hips and her briefs down her legs, as if the bare need between them was the only thing that existed for them, as if it was their lifeline, their reality, and had no need at that moment in time for explanations or pampering or anything to cloud its raw, vital urgency.

Afterwards, though, being Rick, he was tender and funny. He helped her out of her crumpled, wrecked dress, brought her tissues and a glass of water once more, remarked that he suspected he now understood about concupiscence, and held her in his arms and told her extremely improbable stories about his unprintable escapades as a social geographer until she fell asleep.

But next morning he was awake when she woke, watching her, and as he saw the memory of their passion the night before etched starkly in her eyes, he sighed and gathered her close and said, 'Will you marry me?'

CHAPTER NINE

For a long time afterwards, Evonne couldn't understand why those four words had acted as such a catalyst—but nothing altered the fact that they did. The scales fell from her eyes, the confusion lifted from her heart and she suddenly saw it all in brilliant clarity—and knew what she had to do and say.

'Rick——' she hesitated and lifted a hand to touch his face gently, 'you promised me no...steps up the ladder or diamond bracelets.'

'I should have thought this was the opposite,' he said a shade drily.

'If you think offering to make me Lady Emerson isn't a giant step up the ladder...'

'Oh, *that*,' he said dismissively. 'It means nothing. You don't seriously see it like that?' There was a sudden little frown of impatience in his eyes.

'I...in a way, I do,' she said quietly.

'Evonne...'

'No,' she said huskily, 'let me tell you why it would be crazy for us to get married. Firstly there's me...'

'The way you are in bed, if that's what you're still worried about...!'

'It's not. I——' she paused '—with you I could never regret that, and perhaps you've cured me of that anyway.' She stopped again and lowered her lashes so Rick would not see reflected in her eyes the knife of pain going through her heart. 'But,' she looked up steadily, 'there's more of me, there's the side of me you'd find impossible to live with. I think you even realised that last night when you spoke of opposites. Do you know what I was thinking? I was, even then, so soon,' her voice quivered, but she went on resolutely, 'thinking of ways to change you ...'

'You also told me not to change a hair of my head yesterday,' Rick broke in.

'That didn't mean I wouldn't be able to stop myself doing it. I'm like that.'

'You mean, don't you,' he said with a sudden edge, 'that you're still looking for someone to match up to Robert Randall? Someone conventionally powerful, conservative—you've really set your sights high, in other words.'

Three weeks ago, Evonne thought with a pang, that might have been true. Now ... but don't let him get the better of you, Evonne, she thought.

'Then there's you, Rick,' she said swiftly. 'Someone who's bitten off more than they can chew.'

Of all the reactions, laughter was the one she didn't expect, not genuine amusement. 'Oh, I can handle it. Can you?' he queried with gentle mockery then.

Evonne coloured painfully. 'I didn't mean that ...'

'Then you shouldn't say these things unless you mean them,' he pointed out.

She bit her lip. 'I meant ... in an emotional sense. You ... I ...' She stopped, then started again. 'Because you've...*rescued* me, if you like, from the way I was, it doesn't mean to say you have to take responsibility for me and—no, let me finish,' she said sternly. 'Because you're an...honourable person, I think that what's you thought you should do.'

'So,' he said, 'in other words, it would be all right for me to go on sleeping with you until we came to a mutual parting of the ways, but not to want to marry you?'

'No, it wouldn't be all right,' she said huskily. 'I promised myself just one more night, yesterday.'

'One more night?' he said softly, incredulously. 'Just one more night?'

Evonne closed her eyes. 'I...'

'You...? You amaze me, Evonne. Particularly after your one last night. Do you remember any of what you *said* to me last night, outside, when I was kissing you in the moonlight, do you remember...?'

'Rick,' she put in despairingly, 'tell me one thing, did you plan to ask me to marry you this morning or did it just happen because you felt sorry for me?'

He was silent for about a minute. Then he said abruptly, 'No, I hadn't planned to, but...'

'You see?'

Their eyes clashed, and hers were unwittingly hurt but quite determined.

'I...yes, I think I do,' he said at last, and laid his head back on the pillow. 'So you seriously believe this is a passing attraction between us?'

'I...yes,' she whispered.

'All right,' said Rick after another silence, 'perhaps you're right. I shouldn't imagine we've given it much time to prove anything, but if you're so sure I'm not the one for you...'

'I think it's more that I'm not the one for you. I told you that before, but you didn't believe me. You need...'

'Evonne,' he said with sudden violence, 'don't tell me what I need. I'm a little allergic to being told that.'

'Oh, Rick, I'm sorry,' she said helplessly.

'Well,' he sat up and looked down at her, 'at least you haven't told me how sweet I am. How shall we organise this parting of the ways? Any suggestions?'

Evonne curbed an impulse to hide her face in the pillow and wondered vaguely if her heart was bleeding to death. So easy, she marvelled, and you—more fool you—were hoping against hope, weren't you?

'I don't know,' she said barely audibly.

'Yes, it's a pity about that. It would have been better if you could have driven off and left me,' Rick said meditatively, 'but I'm afraid I'll have to take you back to Sydney for your... walking away. But perhaps we can spend our last hours together in friendship of a sort?'

She did bury her face in the pillow then to hide her tears.

'Oh, now, Patterson,' Rick said drily, 'does this mean you don't have the courage of your convictions?'

Evonne twisted her head to look up at him and her eyes were suddenly angry. 'Yes, I do,' she said shortly.

'I think—I hope I do,' he replied

As a parting of the ways their trip to Sydney turned out to be not quite the ordeal Evonne had feared, because Rick acquired a passenger. One of the advertising people called back to Melbourne urgently discovered they were leaving, and when he made his plight known at breakfast Rick offered him a lift as far as Sydney.

In fact it all worked in well, because Evonne had decided to fly straight home from Sydney, so he was able to drop them both off at the airport.

But then again, although she didn't have to pit her wits against Rick's on the drive home, nothing altered or diminished the tearing sensations of pain she felt throughout the trip, the first when she had looked back at Peppers lazing in the morning sunlight, and then at frequent intervals as she thought with a feeble little spark of incredulity how easy it had been.

But that little spark was doused at the airport. Their farewells were stilted until the advertising man took himself off, then they became pointed.

'I . . . got something for you,' Evonne said awkwardly, delving into her hand luggage. 'It's only a bottle of wine, but its the Antique and Wine Company's first vintage, a Peppers Creek Chardonnay. It might be special—they did say to keep it f-for,' her voice cracked, 'a while.'

Rick pulled the bottle out of its brown paper bag and stared at it. 'How appropriate,' he commented. 'In a few years I shall drink it in a moment of sentiment, and toast one of those fleeting encounters of the not-meant-to-be kind. I might even have a suitable wife to wonder at my faraway expression.'

Evonne turned away defensively.

'Tell me one thing,' he said in an oddly hard voice, 'are you still hankering for Robert Randall?'

She turned back and although she was, as always, perfectly groomed, her face was pale and weary. 'No.'

'Just...no?' he said ironically.

'If you don't *want* to believe me what can I say?'

'That you still have a long way to go before you know yourself, Evonne. However, perhaps you're right, only you can sort that out. And all I can do,' he added wryly, 'is take it like a man. Goodbye, my dear Patterson. Thanks for your help with my manuscript and my...' he held up the bottle of wine, 'diamond bracelet.' And he walked away from her without a backward glance.

That night, at home in her apartment, Evonne couldn't sleep and wondered if she ever would again. And the most hurtful of her tortured thoughts, she found, was that Rick believed she was still clinging to that old love. But then, she kept telling herself, what *is* the truth now? That I love Rick as I've never loved before but I *know*

I wouldn't be any good for him. How can I be so sure of both of those things, so certain he didn't really intend marriage? For some reason I had that premise firmly fixed in my mind, but then, when I gave him an escape clause, he took it . . .

If she proved nothing else to herself over the next couple of weeks, she found out how difficult it was to forget Rick. She even, she realised, was hauntingly sad when her period arrived on schedule, although it had only been the faint, crazy hope that something had gone wrong that she had been clinging to.

She took another week off after getting home to Melbourne, then went back to Amos Doubleday.

It was another wet Melbourne morning when she presented herself in his office.

'Evonne!' he exclaimed delightedly, then took a good look at her face and sighed heavily. 'Sit down,' he said gently.

She sat and smoothed her charcoal skirt. 'I've come up with one or two really good ideas for the next catalogue, Amos . . .'

'My dear,' he interrupted, 'please let me say I'm sorry. I shouldn't have done it, and it was only the very real affection and respect I hold you in that prompted me to in the first place.'

Evonne stared at him, then said quietly, 'I believe that, but I'd rather not talk about it.'

'Evonne . . .'

'*Please,*' she whispered, then took a breath. 'Except for one thing. How did you know about Robert Randall?'

'I didn't *know*,' Amos said slowly. 'I put two and two together. When you applied for the job here, I checked your reference personally and, because I knew his grandfather, I was able to speak to him personally. He not only gave you an excellent reference but he also said, "She's not only capable and clever but a rather special person."' He shrugged. 'Over the last two years what had started out as a tiny seed of suspicion in my mind hardened to certainty. I wasn't wrong, was I?'

'No, but he was never in love with me.'

'I see.'

'Well,' Evonne smiled with an effort, 'do you know that coral lends itself to beautiful jewellery when it's polished and that since *Out of Africa* straw sun-hats have achieved a new art form? We're a little behind on the hats, I admit, but I think they're here to stay, and with the milliner I have in mind, who's a modest genius, we could accomplish a range of them to end all ranges, each individually hand-crafted, a label, designer sun-hat and co-ordinated straw bags, perhaps sarongs as well.'

Amos said wryly, 'I see you didn't altogether waste your time in the tropics, Evonne!'

The first note arrived two weeks later, at work.

When she saw the handwriting on the envelope, Evonne's heart started to beat slowly and heavily, her mouth went dry and her hands shook as she tore it open.

> Dear Patterson, Have you noticed that since Peppers the world seems curiously flat? As if one could fall off without trying too hard. Good news re manuscript, by the way—it's been edited and accepted and I can turn my attention to my thesis . . . or I could if I could stop thinking about you. Strange, isn't it, how I seem not to be able to do that since we're so obviously not suited? Rick.

They came twice a week for nearly two months, and Rick employed a technique she knew well, his diary technique, in fact, so she could visualise his day-to-day life, share the books he was reading, the plays and movies he had seen, his often funny political comment. The fact that she didn't answer didn't seem to perturb him. Nor could he have known how close she came to it sometimes, how she began to dread checking her mail in the mornings because it seemed impossible not to do anything, but that was all she was capable of, apparently. How thankful she was that she had a well-trained secretary who never opened any private mail—which was just as well. Her maidenly soul would have been sorely embarrassed at some of the memories Rick evoked so vividly. And he couldn't have known the sense of utter confusion that was mounting in Evonne, the questions she asked herself . . .

Then they ceased abruptly, and she went from dreading the mail to lying sleepless at night wondering, hoping against hope that there would be one on her desk the next morning.

A week after their cessation, Amos press-ganged her into going home with him for dinner. 'You're looking thin and ragged,' he accused her. 'You, my living advertisement!'

'Amos, if this is . . .'

'It's not. Hattie says she hasn't seen you for ages!' He stared at her reproachfully.

'Well—but . . .'

'No buts!'

Hattie Doubleday might get a knitting pattern confused, but if there was one thing she loved it was cooking, at which she excelled.

'Oh, dear,' Evonne said helplessly, a three-course meal later and as she stared at a silver dish of brandy snaps, 'I'll burst if I eat another thing!'

Hattie rolled her eyes heavenwards. 'I know it's fashionable to be thin, but you can take it too far. Remember that,' she said, and patted Evonne's hand kindly. 'Now tell me some more about this new range Amos seems so excited about—coral jewellery, hats and bags.'

Evonne obliged, and produced preliminary photos of what they had chosen for the catalogue.

'Beautiful!' sighed Hattie. 'If only I was slim enough to wear a sarong . . . what have I said?' she enquired as Amos and Evonne grinned at each other.

They told her, and she laughed richly. She was a happy, kind-hearted person—what a pity she couldn't have children, Evonne thought with a sudden pang.

And right on cue, Hattie patted her person, searched a pocket, then said with a shrug, 'I seem to have lost it, but I got a letter from Ricky today, Amos. You would not believe what that poor boy...'

'Hattie!' muttered Amos, and pulled a peculiar face which his wife seemed not to notice, because she went on,

'Not that you could have read it, his writing is bad enough at the best of times, but I suppose I've had years of practice.' She turned to Evonne. 'But I'm forgetting—you know our nephew, don't you? Amos sent you up to help him with his manuscript, and he certainly asked to be remembered to you in his letter—at least I'm pretty sure it was that. Such a talented boy, isn't he?' she sighed. 'Imagine, one day he'll be Dr Sir Richard Emerson! If only he weren't so accident-prone...'

Evonne looked across at Amos, her eyes cold, and he sent her a helpless little shrug in return, but then they both turned to Hattie and echoed simultaneously, 'Accident-prone?'

'You wouldn't believe what's happened this time! He was driving his car—I never liked the idea of that Porsche, Amos, they go so wickedly fast, but he *says* he wasn't in the wrong—when someone ran into him! A truck, would you believe!'

'Hattie!' Amos said urgently.

But Hattie continued soothingly, 'It's only his .rm that's broken—an ankle last time, this time an arm. He says he's sure this period of his life is closed now, because these things come in threes—two limbs and his car is pretty broken up, but the really sad part of it...'

Amos rose quietly and fetched Evonne a brandy. 'Drink it,' he said gently.

She did, coughed a little as Hattie talked on, seemingly unaware. And when she finally spoke it was to say incredulously to Hattie, 'You mean to say he lost *all* his notes for his thesis in this accident?'

'Not quite all.'

'But how?'

'They got run over.'

Evonne closed her eyes. 'It's not possible!'

'Nothing's impossible with Rick,' Hattie said placidly. 'He had, you see, a briefcase in his car, containing his notes and part of a typescript of his thesis, plus the *copy*. Well, in the collision, the door flew open, the briefcase flew out and also flew open and under the wheels of the truck. If this wasn't bad enough, a fire engine arrived to spray the truck with some sort of foam because it was carrying an inflammable load, and no one realised that all the paper lying around was Ricky's thesis.' Hattie shook her head sadly. 'He reckons it will be a little while yet before he'll be Dr Sir Richard, some of his work is irre-placeable without doing another trip, and anyway, it was his left arm he broke. Evonne, my dear child, what's wrong?'

Later, as Amos escorted Evonne to her car, he said, 'I *swear* I knew nothing about this!'

'Forgive me, but I don't believe you... The timing, for one thing.'

'Evonne...'

But she rounded on him and said bitterly, 'If you ever interfere in my life again, Amos, I'll never speak to you *again*!' And she got into her car, dropped her face briefly into her hands, then drove off with a roar.

'Hattie,' Amos said sternly, 'that was extremely bad of you—and you always were a clever girl,' he added tenderly. 'But is it all true?'

'Of course it's true! I got the letter this very morning! Why do you think I made you invite her to dinner?'

Evonne couldn't get a flight that night, it was too late, so she said to herself, that's a good thing. I can sleep on it, not do anything rash. Was there ever a letter? Or was it just Amos and Hattie's machinations? What if there wasn't even an accident and they made it all up? I'll look a right fool running up to Sydney... but would they do something like that?

'Yes, they would,' she told herself. 'Remember how Amos conned you into going to Brampton in the first place? Well, I won't fall for the same card trick twice!'

She was home by this time, pacing her apartment like an angry tigress. She had changed into a long scarlet silky robe and removed her make-up; she was incredibly angry and wrought-up and there was no way she was going to be able to sleep, she knew.

But Rick did stop writing, she reminded herself, although who's to say it wasn't because I didn't answer? Why didn't I?

She stalked across to her writing desk and got all his notes out of a drawer—and re-read every one of them, then held them to her breast. Love letters? she asked herself with a tortured look in her eyes. In Rick's own inimitable manner, but could they be classed as love letters? He doesn't actually *say* it, but why would *he* feel as if the world had gone flat and you could fall off rather easily if he wasn't...he isn't... And all the other little things he says, the dozens of ways he's made me part of his life—this house he's renting, for example, in Woollahra...that's a big jump from Woolloomooloo—what am I thinking!

Why is it always raining in Sydney when I fly in? Evonne asked herself the next morning as she stared out of the taxi. What will Amos be thinking right now? Serves him right if he's wondering whether I've been run over by a bus!

'Woollahra, you say,' the taxi driver broke into her thoughts. 'What's the street again? Doesn't ring a bell.'

'Well, haven't you got a map or something?'

'It's a bit difficult to drive and read a map at the same time.'

'I thought taxi drivers were supposed to...'

'Sydney's a big city, lady. I'll have to stop and ask.'

In all he had to stop three times, during which process Evonne's nerves stretched to screaming point. So that when they finally found the street and the house she said bitterly as she paid him, 'I can tell you, you wouldn't get a licence in Melbourne!' causing the driver to look at her sardonically and drive off in a similar manner.

'Damn!' she muttered to herself, hastily raising her fold-up umbrella which she always travelled with. 'I don't even know if he's home, for all I know he might still be in hospital or heaven knows where! I should have asked the taxi to wait.' She grimaced angrily.

She looked distractedly up and down the quiet, leafy street and knew that if Rick wasn't home she would have to walk up to a main road to get another taxi. She looked down at her elegant black leather pumps, at the rain hissing down on to the pavement all around her, splashing her shoes and tights, at her sombre grey suit and white blouse, at her fingers clutching her black purse so tightly, then finally at the street door let into a high wall, standing slightly ajar, and she drew a trembling breath.

The doorway led into a small, tiled courtyard with plants in pots, all dripping in the rain. The front door of the two-storey, narrow, lovely old house was also ajar, she saw, and she hesitated, then crossed the courtyard swiftly, snapped her umbrella shut, hung it on a stand that bore another one beneath the small porch roof, and stepped inside.

The front door opened right into a lounge that was two steps down, a lounge decorated in sandy beige with dark leather furniture, pictures on the rough brick feature wall, slimline blinds on the windows, modern lamps lending a welcoming glow from the gloom outside.

And Rick. Sitting on the floor surrounded by papers. Rick in a blue and green football jersey with a white collar, and jeans, Rick barefooted and with his sun-streaked hair ruffled and falling over his eyes as he looked up. Rick with one sleeve of the football jersey cut off raggedly above the elbow and a plaster cast down to his fingers. Rick, staring, then blinking experimentally.

And herself, unable to tear her eyes away from his, unable to believe the torrent of emotion rising in her...

CHAPTER TEN

'*EVONNE!*'

But incredibly, Evonne heard herself saying hysterically, 'Don't imagine I don't know why you've done this! So that you could blackmail me into crawling through crocodile-infested swamps and creeks with you while you get your thesis together again. Don't think...' But she was shaking and crying and it was impossible to go on.

Until she saw Rick get up awkwardly and come towards her, then all her fears and uncertainties spilled out again. 'You think you know me, but you *don't*. I'd be the very worst wife for you...'

'You can change me all you like,' he offered.

'But I can't change *me*. Don't you understand—I'm possessive, jealous and dictatorial, I can be bitchy and moody and I'll probably have a chip on my shoulder until the day I *die*!'

'If you think I'm perfect...'

But she went on as if he hadn't spoken, 'I'd be utterly miserable... socially and culturally geographing with you, but I'd be scared stiff to let you out of my sight—I *know* about all the little Swiss girls, don't forget.'

'I won't do any more socialling or culturalling in the field, but if I had you, you could let me loose safely in a b... well, in a beauty pageant.'

'If you meant a brothel why didn't you say it!' she snapped.

Rick smiled down at her and abruptly all the fight went out of Evonne—she went weak inside, weak with longing and a hunger and thirst that seemed to know no bounds. 'But you left me,' her lips trembled, 'you walked away, you talked about someone *else*...matching me, you told me you'd asked me to marry you on the spur of the moment...'

'I did, but only because I got over-eager, like a horse rushing his fences—basically I knew it was too soon to ask you that and I'd planned to wait. But then again it was instrumental in making me see what I had to do—I had to let you walk away from me. The time had come, my love, to leave the ball in your court. If——' he paused, 'I wasn't very nice about it, it was because while I knew I had to do it, I was also petrified I might lose you,' he said softly, and put his good arm around her very gently.

'Oh,' she whispered, remembering suddenly the things he had said that last morning and understanding at last. 'If nothing else proves to you what a fool I am, surely that must?'

'All it proves is that you came back of your own free will.'

'No—well, I had some help. Hattie and Amos contrived to let me know about the accident.'

Rick ran his fingers up the back of her neck and through her hair, somewhat disordering the neat knot it was in.

'But you put yourself on a plane, I presume?'

'Yes...and fought with a taxi driver.' Evonne closed her eyes and leant her head on his shoulder. 'Rick...I'm scared,' she whispered. 'So scared of the way you make me feel, so afraid of what I'll do to the way *you* feel...smother it, crush it...I'm not good at handling...'

He put his fingers under her chin and made her look up at him and caressed her mouth for a moment, then he said, 'Do you believe in me at all?'

'I——' she swallowed, 'I believe in you more than anything. It's *me*...'

'Then all you have to do is trust me. Will you marry me, Evonne?'

She stared into his eyes, so green and steady, then she sighed helplessly. 'Yes.'

Rick bent his head and kissed her lips. 'I think I have to sit down,' he murmured, and rocked slightly so that she clutched him anxiously.

'What is it?'

'The world seemed to move, but I also,' he paused as they moved towards a settee and sank on to it, 'have to be honest and confess to you that I'm slightly incapacitated.'

'I know that,' she glanced at his cast, 'but...'

'There's more, I'm afraid. I rather severely grazed a hip and ricked my back and cut myself in a...really awkward spot—oh, nothing that won't heal completely in time, in fact I'm a hell of a lot better already, but I've been warned off— well, sex, for a little while...I'm glad you can laugh about it,' he added with utter false gravity as Evonne buried her face in his football jumper and laughed until she cried.

*   *   *

They were married a week later, a week they spent together, but platonically on account of Rick's injuries—if you could call the way they touched, the time they spent in each other's arms, platonic.

It had its advantages, he said frequently, it was a true period of courtship—to which Evonne replied once that indeed it was, and did he like onion chopped into his spinach?

She took him to see her mother, who was utterly bowled over and rendered almost speechless when she realised her eldest daughter was to be a Lady, then recovered sufficiently to immediately want to organise a gathering of the clan. Evonne started to demur, but Rick said he would be delighted and why not make it a wedding party?

'Are you ashamed of me,' he asked her later, 'or your family?'

She blushed and set her teeth, then told him the truth—she couldn't quite believe this was happening to her, she told him, which was why it seemed better not to let too many people in on it.

'Believe it,' he said gently.

Evonne thought for a while, then told him he had better get in touch with Amos and Hattie and invite them up, and since she was now doing the laundry, would he mind clearing his pockets himself, because she thought she had already washed some notes.

Rick replied that taking over the housekeeping while he was recuperating was something he was very grateful for but to rest assured he believed in equality in those matters and would muck in and do his bit once they were married and once all his disabilities had healed—two things which he *hoped*, he said, would occur concurrently. Evonne surveyed him and muttered, Heaven help us!

And the days slipped by, wet mostly, so they were wrapped in their own little world, insulated by the heavy skies and drenching rain.

Then there was only one day to go, and Amos and Hattie descended on them. Hattie insisted that Evonne must spend the night with them at their hotel, that it was supremely unlucky for a bride to see her bridegroom the night before the wedding—and Evonne's mother turned up at that point and was equally adamant.

Evonne hesitated, then gave in, and after a jolly lunch they bore her away, leaving Amos to console Rick. In fact, she spent the night with her mother, but only after an exhausting shopping trip which those two determined ladies forced her on—Hattie and her mother were obviously kindred spirits and quite shocked to find she had made no preparations for her wedding at all. 'I've already got an outfit,' she insisted— Hattie had brought her some clothes to add to the meagre supply she had been forced to go out and buy after leaving Melbourne in only what she stood up in. 'The ivory silk suit you brought for me will be perfect, Hattie, and *no*, I swear I've never worn it before!'

Well, underwear then, they insisted, a nightgown to end all nightgowns—and flowers! She couldn't be married without flowers, surely?

Evonne gave in at that point, mainly because of the look in her mother's eyes

But not even that look could stop her lying awake half the night, staring into the darkness and thinking, I should never have let them take me away from him... Do I have the courage to go through with this?

She switched on the bedside lamp and looked around. It was not any of the series of slum houses she had grown up in—years before she had helped her mother move to a better suburb, and with Sam and Sandra at home but both working and with what Evonne still insisted on contributing and the others when they could, it was pleasant and homely, but still a long way from Woollahra.

'And baronets, however improbable, and estates in England—I'll probably discover that by elderly he means it's a national treasure— and... and I'm scared again!'

She got up at first light and stole out of the house to find a clear dawn breaking. Glory be, she thought, Hattie and Mum were no doubt also worried about that other old superstition—happy the bride the sun shines on. But, she mused as she wandered down the deserted street, is there going to be a bride and a wedding today?

It was her mother who helped her make the decision. Her mother who was up and waiting for her with a pot of tea made, who sat across the kitchen table from her as she sipped it and watched her carefully. Her mother with her lined face and knobbly fingers from years of doing other people's washing and ironing, cleaning and scrubbing their floors, who said, 'You have to have faith in something, Evonne.'

'I don't know how you of all people can say that,' she whispered.

'If I'd had no faith, pet, I'd have taken the easy way out. I'd have put some of you in foster-homes and told myself no one could blame me—which would have been true, and I'm not saying it's not the right way for some, but it wasn't for me. I *believed* you were best with me, I never lost faith in that. Was I wrong?'

Evonne got up swiftly and went round to kneel at her mother's side. 'Oh, darling, no! If I've ever... forgive me if I've ever let you think that.' She laid her head on her mother's lap. 'I'm only sorry I always wanted to get away, but...' She stopped helplessly.

Her mother smiled wisely and smoothed her hair. 'I'm not,' she said softly. 'It was only natural and right, and I'm so proud of you. But now's the time to *really* believe in yourself, because if you can't, then you might as well have stayed.'

'He...' Evonne stopped again.

'He loves you, Evonne.'

'Can you see it? How?'

'I can see the weight of it in you,' her mother said slowly. 'Do you love him?'

'Too much, I'm afraid.'

'He's no fool, though. I think he knows you very well. Look, I can't promise you'll be happy ever afterwards, nobody can promise you that, but *everybody* takes that risk, not just you, so have a little faith.'

*   *   *

Between Amos and Hattie, Evonne's mother and all her delighted brothers and sisters, their wedding breakfast after the register office ceremony turned out to be a happy affair. If the bride looked a little shell-shocked, she was also stunningly beautiful in her simple ivory silk suit, pale stockings and with a bouquet of violets. If the groom was not quite as talkative as normal, he was certainly more formally dressed than normal in a lightweight beautifully tailored grey suit, navy tie and pale blue shirt. In other aspects he hadn't changed much—half-way to the register office he had decided categorically that he had left the wedding ring at home, and only by sheer force had his exasperated uncle wrested it out of his shirt pocket, flourished it in his face and then decided he had better keep it.

But none of the wedding breakfast party noticed any deficiencies in the bridal pair, and several of them, particularly Amos Doubleday, looked positively smug now the deed was actually done. As for Evonne's family, they were so spontaneously happy for her, so obviously enjoying this surprise event, so naïvely thrilled that their eldest sister was now Lady Emerson, they brought tears to her eyes.

Then it was time to leave, and when someone asked Rick where they were going on their honeymoon and he hesitated, then said he hadn't actually thought about it, everyone laughed uproariously.

But in the taxi they took back to Woollahra, not a great deal was said.

'I hardly recognise you in that suit. Did you buy it specially?' Evonne asked.

'Uncle Amos brought it with him, and the shirt and tie.'

'Oh.'

'I feel a real fool,' Rick admitted.

'Oh?'

'I mean about the honeymoon. We haven't done much forward planning at all, have we?'

'No. No, we haven't.'

They were silent for the rest of the way, but once inside his house, Evonne stood for a moment in the middle of the lounge, then turned to him suddenly. 'What's wrong? Aren't you feeling well?'

'No,' he said very quietly, and came over to her to take her hand. 'Reaction, I guess, but this will help.' He put his arms around her and stared into her eyes, then suddenly buried his face in her shoulder and held her so hard she could barely breathe.

'Rick,' she whispered, 'what is it? Tell me.'

'I thought you wouldn't...do it. When they took you away from me yesterday, I thought...I might never see you again. I've been feeling sick inside all night, sick and desperate, and even now as if it hasn't really happened.'

Evonne closed her eyes and said shakily, 'Does it mean so much to you?'

'More than you'll ever know, perhaps. I love you, Evonne, and it started not long after I met you, I'm afraid—there just doesn't seem to be anything I can do about it. Hell, I think I need a drink. I feel like passing out.' Rick raised his head at last and he was so unusually pale that her lips parted.

Then she tilted her head back and kissed him gently and said huskily, 'Oh, Rick, I love you. I'm sorry... only I could have been such a fool, and...'

'Don't, my darling!'

'I was only going to say... and please don't pass out on me now, because I want to keep saying I love you and showing you...'

It was some time before she got the opportunity to talk any more at all, as they held each other in final understanding and, at last, totally united.

Then Evonne remembered how pale Rick had looked and she said, 'Come,' and led him to the settee, helped him take his jacket off over his cast, then fetched them both brandies.

'On top of champagne this might—who knows?' said Rick ruefully. 'But I don't think I need restoring any more.'

'I think I'd better be the judge of that,' she said softly.

He looked at her meditatively, some of the old amusement back in his eyes. 'I thought you'd brought me here to show me something?'

'When I'm quite sure you're up to it, yes,' she replied innocently.

'Apart from this wretched thing,' he held up his broken arm, 'I'm fine now—Evonne, you're not planning to stop me making love to you on our wedding day, are you?' He stared at her in serious alarm.

She snuggled against him.

'I can manage with this, I promise. An arm is, after all, not the most vital...well...'

'Hush!' she said, veiling the laughter in her eyes. 'Don't look so tormented. It's just that out of consideration for your other sore areas, *I* was planning to make love to *you*, but then I did promise myself, having taken this momentous step, that I wouldn't run true to form and be dictatorial so early on at least, and if...'

'Perish the thought!' Rick broke in. 'Dictate all you like—I've got the feeling I'm going to love it.'

Which, later, he did.

Harlequin Presents®

Coming Next Month

From *New York Times* Bestselling author
Penny Jordan, a compelling novel of ruthless passion
that will mesmerize readers everywhere!

PennyJordan

Silver

Real power, true power came from
Rothwell. And Charles vowed to have it,
the earldom and all that went with it.

Silver vowed to destroy Charles, just as surely and
uncaringly as he had destroyed her father; just as he had
intended to destroy her. She needed him to want her . . .
to desire her . . . until he'd do anything to have her.

But first she needed a tutor: a man who wanted no one.
He would help her bait the trap.

Played out on a glittering international stage,
Silver's story leads her from the luxurious comfort of
British aristocracy into the depths of adventure,
passion and danger.

AVAILABLE IN OCTOBER!

 HARLEQUIN

From America's favorite author
coming in September

JANET DAILEY

For Bitter Or Worse
Out of print since 1979!

Reaching Cord seemed impossible. Bitter, still confined to a wheelchair a year after the crash, he lashed out at everyone. Especially his wife.

"It would have been better if I hadn't been pulled from the plane wreck," he told her, and nothing Stacey did seemed to help.

Then Paula Hanson, a confident physiotherapist, arrived. She taunted Cord into helping himself, restoring his interest in living. Could she also make him and Stacey rediscover their early love?

Don't miss this collector's edition—last in a special three-book collection from Janet Dailey.

Take 4 bestselling love stories FREE

Plus get a FREE surprise gift!

PASSPORT TO ROMANCE
SWEEPSTAKES RULES

1. **HOW TO ENTER:** To enter, you must be the age of majority and complete the official entry form, or print your name, address, telephone number and age on a plain piece of paper and mail to: Passport to Romance, P.O. Box 9056, Buffalo, NY 14269-9056. No mechanically reproduced entries accepted.

2. All entries must be received by the CONTEST CLOSING DATE, DECEMBER 31, 1990 TO BE ELIGIBLE.

3. **THE PRIZES:** There will be ten (10) Grand Prizes awarded, each consisting of a choice of a trip for two people from the following list:
   i) London, England (approximate retail value $5,050 U.S.)
   ii) England, Wales and Scotland (approximate retail value $6,400 U.S.)
   iii) Carribean Cruise (approximate retail value $7,300 U.S.)
   iv) Hawaii (approximate retail value $9,550 U.S.)
   v) Greek Island Cruise in the Mediterranean (approximate retail value $12,250 U.S.)
   vi) France (approximate retail value $7,300 U.S.)

4. Any winner may choose to receive any trip or a cash alternative prize of $5,000.00 U.S. in lieu of the trip.

5. **GENERAL RULES:** Odds of winning depend on number of entries received.

6. A random draw will be made by Nielsen Promotion Services, an independent judging organization, on January 29, 1991, in Buffalo, NY, at 11:30 a.m. from all eligible entries received on or before the Contest Closing Date.

7. Any Canadian entrants who are selected must correctly answer a time-limited, mathematical skill-testing question in order to win.

8. Full contest rules may be obtained by sending a stamped, self-addressed envelope to: "Passport to Romance Rules Request", P.O. Box 9998, Saint John, New Brunswick, Canada E2L 4N4.

9. Quebec residents may submit any litigation respecting the conduct and awarding of a prize in this contest to the Régie des loteries et courses du Québec.

10. Payment of taxes other than air and hotel taxes is the sole responsibility of the winner.

11. Void where prohibited by law.

COUPON BOOKLET OFFER TERMS

To receive your Free travel-savings coupon booklets, complete the mail-in Offer Certificate on the preceeding page, including the necessary number of proofs-of-purchase, and mail to: Passport to Romance, P.O. Box 9057, Buffalo, NY 14269-9057. The coupon booklets include savings on travel-related products such as car rentals, hotels, cruises, flowers and restaurants. Some restrictions apply. The offer is available in the United States and Canada. Requests must be postmarked by January 25, 1991. Only proofs-of-purchase from specially marked "Passport to Romance" Harlequin® or Silhouette® books will be accepted. The offer certificate must accompany your request and may not be reproduced in any manner. Offer void where prohibited or restricted by law. LIMIT FOUR COUPON BOOKLETS PER NAME, FAMILY, GROUP, ORGANIZATION OR ADDRESS. Please allow up to 8 weeks after receipt of order for shipment. Enter quickly as quantities are limited. Unfulfilled mail-in offer requests will receive free Harlequin® or Silhouette® books (not previously available in retail stores), in quantities equal to the number of proofs-of-purchase required for Levels One to Four, as applicable.

PR-SWPS

OFFICIAL SWEEPSTAKES ENTRY FORM

Complete and return this Entry Form immediately—the more Entry Forms you submit, the better your chances of winning!
- Entry Forms must be received by **December 31, 1990**
- A random draw will take place on **January 29, 1991**
- Trip must be taken by **December 31, 1991**

3-HP-1-SW

YES, I want to win a PASSPORT TO ROMANCE vacation for two! I understand the prize includes round-trip air fare, accommodation and a daily spending allowance.

Name_____

Address_____

City_____ State_____ Zip_____

Telephone Number_____ Age_____

Return entries to: **PASSPORT TO ROMANCE**, P.O. Box 9056, Buffalo, NY 14269-9056

© 1990 Harlequin Enterprises Limited

COUPON BOOKLET/OFFER CERTIFICATE

Item	LEVEL ONE Booklet 1	LEVEL TWO Booklet 1 & 2	LEVEL THREE Booklet 1, 2 & 3	LEVEL FOUR Booklet 1, 2, 3 & 4
Booklet 1 = $100+	$100+	$100+	$100+	$100+
Booklet 2 = $200+		$200+	$200+	$200+
Booklet 3 = $300+			$300+	$300+
Booklet 4 = $400+	____	____	____	$400+
Approximate Total Value of Savings	$100+	$300+	$600+	$1,000+
# of Proofs of Purchase Required	4	6	12	18
Check One	____	____	____	____

Name_____

Address_____

City_____ State_____ Zip_____

Return Offer Certificates to: **PASSPORT TO ROMANCE**, P.O. Box 9057, Buffalo, NY 14269-9057

Requests must be postmarked by **January 25, 1991**

✂--

ONE PROOF OF PURCHASE

3-HP-1

To collect your free coupon booklet you must include the necessary number of proofs-of-purchase with a properly completed Offer Certificate

© 1990 Harlequin Enterprises Limited

See previous page for details